12/01

SURVIVAL INSTINCT

Fargo was about to mount when the Ovaro suddenly shied away. Fargo knew better than to ignore the horse's reaction, so he threw himself to the side as an arrow thwacked into the saddle, where his head had been an instant before.

He rolled and came to his knees, the long blade of the Arkansas toothpick pointed directly into the shadows that billowed, grew, and then exploded as a burly Sioux warrior charged out, bow and arrow abandoned in favor of a war club raised high above his head. He bowled Fargo over, but Fargo was ready and grabbed the brave.

With a furious war cry, the brave swung his war club at Fargo's skull just as Fargo thrust upward with his knife, aiming for the Sioux's heart. . . .

THE TRAILSMAN

#242

WYOMING WHIRLWIND

by

Jon Sharpe

A SIGNET BOOK

SIGNET
Published by New American Library, a division of
Penguin Putnam Inc., 375 Hudson Street,
New York, New York 10014, U.S.A.
Penguin Books Ltd, 80 Strand,
London WC2R 0RL, England
Penguin Books Australia Ltd, Ringwood,
Victoria, Australia
Penguin Books Canada Ltd, 10 Alcorn Avenue,
Toronto, Ontario, Canada M4V 3B2
Penguin Books (N.Z.) Ltd, 182–190 Wairau Road,
Auckland 10, New Zealand

Penguin Books Ltd, Registered Offices:
Harmondsworth, Middlesex, England

First published by Signet, an imprint of New American Library,
a division of Penguin Putnam Inc.

First Printing, December 2001
10 9 8 7 6 5 4 3 2 1

The first chapter of this book previously appeared in *Texas Blood Money*,
the two hundred forty-first volume in this series.

 REGISTERED TRADEMARK—MARCA REGISTRADA

Printed in the United States of America

PUBLISHER'S NOTE
This is a work of fiction. Names, characters, places, and incidents either are
the product of the author's imagination or are used fictitiously, and any
resemblance to actual persons, living or dead, events, or locales is entirely
coincidental.

The Trailsman

Beginnings . . . they bend the tree and they mark the man. Skye Fargo was born when he was eighteen. Terror was his midwife, vengeance his first cry. Killing spawned Skye Fargo, ruthless, cold-blooded murder. Out of the acrid smoke of gunpowder still hanging in the air, he rose, cried out a promise never forgotten.

The Trailsman they began to call him all across the West: searcher, scout, hunter, the man who could see where others only looked, his skills for hire but not his soul, the man who lived each day to the fullest, yet trailed each tomorrow. Skye Fargo, the Trailsman, the seeker who could take the wildness of a land and the wanting of a woman and make them his own.

Wyoming, 1859—
Death makes good on but one promise:
Both the rich and poor
shall see it kept.

1

Thunder Basin in eastern Wyoming had never looked more deserted. The vast grasslands stretched to the horizon like a green, endlessly heaving ocean. Skye Fargo drew rein and dismounted to give his stallion a rest. He swiped at the sweat beading his forehead as he studied the expanse in front of him for sign of a buffalo herd. Killing one of the big wooly beasts provided more meat than he needed, but it was an easier kill than going after the wily rabbits that poked out their long-eared heads from hidden burrows, then lit out faster than a bullet could follow.

Fargo figured to kill a buffalo, eat his fill, and dress out the rest. He wasn't all that far from Newcastle and could sell the meat there for another month of supplies.

"I want water, too," he said to his Ovaro, patting the horse on the neck. The stallion tossed its head and tried to rear. This unusual behavior put Fargo on guard. When he saw the horse's nostrils flare and the whites around its eyes show, he knew something was seriously amiss.

Hand resting on the Colt holstered at his side, Fargo turned his sharp eyes out across the gently waving grasslands. Thunder Basin was not living up to its name. For three days Fargo had ridden without spotting so much as a cloud above the increasingly sere grass. He had seen drier stretches, but not recently. There had to be something more than a storm cloud randomly tossing off lightning he could not see or hear that spooked the normally steady horse.

Fargo smelled the prairie fire before he saw it.

A cold chill ran down his spine. Indians and outlaws

held no terror for him. He had faced grizzly bears and had walked away. Blizzards and wind storms did not frighten him unduly. They were natural occurrences, however violent, and a smart man survived them. But not a prairie fire. They took on a life of their own, devouring everything in their path. Worst of all for anyone trapped on the prairie, the path of the fire could change on a dime. One instant the fire might be burning east. A gust of wind might set it burning north faster than any man could escape—or the fire could double back over terrain it had already charred, as if leery of leaving a single blade of grass untouched.

Skye Fargo was known as the Trailsman because of his skills, but even the Trailsman wisely gave way before a prairie fire. The only safe place when the fires raced with the wind across a broad grassland was far, far away.

Fargo mounted and turned his paint's face away from the greasy gray smoke he spotted on the horizon to the north. The smell of burning vegetation filled his nostrils now and mingled with it came another unmistakable odor—burned meat. The buffalos he had sought must have been caught in the fire as well.

Casting a quick look over his shoulder to locate the herd brought Fargo up short. In the distance he spotted a lone rider.

"Damnation," he muttered. Fargo tugged on the Ovaro's reins and got the horse headed back in the direction they had been traveling before he had scented the fire. The horse balked, but Fargo kept it moving down the gently sloping hill and out across Thunder Basin.

Fargo put his heels to the horse's flanks, urging as much speed as he could from the powerful animal. He kept his head down but looked up now and again to be sure he headed in the proper direction. Huge walls of billowing black smoke rose on his right, getting closer but still not an immediate threat.

"Turn back!" Fargo shouted. "Fire! Look behind you!"

The rider straightened and looked around as if shaken out of deep thought. Then he reined in.

"Hello," the man called. "What did you say?"

"Fire!" shouted Fargo. He pointed frantically. The advancing wall of roiling smoke now showed faint specks of bright orange and yellow flames in its midst. The fire was still miles off, but Fargo knew how fast a prairie fire moved.

Faster than a horse could ever hope to run.

"What? What's that?" The man seemed too bull-headed to acknowledge what was obvious to Fargo.

Fargo pointed toward the unmistakable wall of smoke now laced with bright tongues of flame. The wind was picking up and blew directly at the man's back. Fargo might have been safe if he had not seen the rider and come to warn him. But he would never have slept well again if he had abandoned the man to his fate.

"We have to get out of the path of the fire. It'll kill everything in its path."

"Fire? I thought that was a thunderstorm. It's been so dry, I reckoned on getting a little wet."

"You're going to get a lot burned unless you hightail it now," Fargo said, coming up beside the man. He gave the rider a quick once-over and wondered what he had found out here in the basin. The man's clothing was impeccably clean and looked brand-new—store-bought new. He wore his fancy beaver felt hat pulled down at a jaunty angle on his forehead. There was hardly enough dust on the broad brim for the hat to have been out of the box longer than a day or two. Shiny boots with flashy patterns gleamed in the gathering smoke, and riding at the man's hip was a Smith & Wesson that had never been fired.

"I suppose we should get out of the way of the fire, then," the man said. He twisted around and thrust out his hand. "My name's Paul Hancock."

"Mine's Fargo. Now ride like you mean it." Fargo hesitated a moment, then asked. "You *can* ride?"

"Why, of course I can," Hancock said, irritated. "I can ride as good as you, I am sure. Although that is a mighty fine specimen of horseflesh you're astride."

Fargo looked at him as if he lost his senses. He stood in the stirrups and got a look at the countryside. Continuing in the direction Hancock had been riding would mean their deaths within the hour. Fargo knew he could never retrace his path to the rise. That was all uphill and his Ovaro, strong as it was, had tired racing across the grassland to reach Paul Hancock.

"That way," Fargo said, coming to a quick decision. The terrain sloped downward slightly, possibly draining into a stream. If so, that gave them even better protection against the fire devouring the grasslands to the east. The fire might jump a small stream, but if the land drained into a river, they were safe after they crossed it.

"What's in that direction?" Hancock asked, still not acknowledging the danger they faced. Fargo already imagined the heat turning his six-shooter too hot to touch, his shirt smoldering, his flesh turning red and then blistering.

"If we're lucky, a river," Fargo said. "If we're not lucky in finding water, we still might escape."

"Why such a hurry?" Hancock asked as Fargo galloped off.

Fargo looked over his shoulder as he rode and wondered if he would have to rope and hogtie Hancock to get him out of danger. The man was totally oblivious to everything happening around him. Fargo had seen toddlers with better sense than the fancy-dressed man.

He heaved a sigh of relief when he saw Hancock snap the reins and get his mare into a trot. When it became apparent Fargo was leaving him farther behind by the minute, Hancock pulled the new hat down around his ears and spurred his horse into a gallop.

Fargo knew the danger of running across a grassy stretch like this. Prairie-dog holes, rabbit burrows, snake holes . . . all afforded excellent ways for a horse barreling along to break a leg. It was a risk he had to take now if he wanted to keep his hide from being roasted like a pheasant on a cooking spit.

"This is great fun!" called Hancock, pulling even with Fargo. The man's horse was fresher, not having galloped miles out onto the prairie to warn a damned fool of the danger. Fargo was glad he had not simply fired a warning shot but had come to fetch the man. Hancock would have ignored gunfire, thinking it was nothing but thunder from a nonexistent storm. How anyone could be so ignorant and still be alive was beyond Fargo.

He hunkered down and knew the Ovaro would carry him to safety. The fire was no longer overtaking them. By riding at an angle to the fire line, he took a chance, but the downhill slope made the effort easier for the paint.

A loud cry of surprise followed by a sound that turned Fargo sick inside forced him to slow the Ovaro's retreat, then circle and backtrack.

Paul Hancock lay flat on his back staring up at the smoky sky. His chest heaved as he struggled to catch his breath. He had been thrown from his horse and had had the wind knocked from his lungs. Otherwise, he appeared all right.

The horse wasn't as lucky. Fargo had heard the sound a horse's leg breaking too often not to recognize it instantly. The whinnying and frightened snorts completed the sad story. He had worried about his horse stepping into a hole. Hancock's had. Whether the other man had been too inexperienced to avoid the prairie-dog hole or had not seen it in his rush to keep up with Fargo hardly mattered.

"Wh-what happened?" Hancock asked, struggling to sit up.

"Your horse broke its leg," Fargo said. "You want to handle it?" He studied the man for a moment and couldn't tell if the fall had shaken him up so much he didn't understand or if he simply was faced with a situation beyond his experience. There wasn't time to discuss it.

Fargo drew his Colt, aimed, and fired. The bullet took down the pain-racked horse instantly, putting it out of its misery.

"You shot my horse!" shouted Hancock, fumbling for his Smith & Wesson.

"You looked too shook up to do it yourself," Fargo said. "Climb up behind me."

"My gear," Hancock said, stumbling forward.

"It'll get burned up with both of us if you don't mount fast." Fargo held out his hand for Hancock. The man returned his six-shooter to its holster and let Fargo help him up. The Ovaro staggered slightly under the doubled weight, then took off with its usual even gait.

"How can you be so sure the fire will come this way?" Hancock asked.

"You can see it, feel it, smell it, and taste it," Fargo said. He brought the Ovaro to a trot and kept it at this gait because any faster would exhaust it. The last thing Fargo wanted was to be afoot on the prairie with a fire burning the flesh at the back of his neck.

"Oh," was all Hancock said. The man fell silent as they made their way at an angle to the fire. By the time they reached the dubious safety of the small stream, the crackle and snap of flames were easily heard.

"Rest for a few minutes," Fargo ordered the man. "Get yourself wet all over. I don't think the fire will jump the stream, but there's no reason not to give ourselves whatever advantage we can." He let his pinto drink while he walked into the knee-deep stream and then sat, taking care to hold his Colt above water as he dunked himself.

Hancock was slower to follow suit and, when he did join Fargo, forgot to draw his Smith & Wesson. He didn't notice that he had given his black-powder gun such a dousing that it probably would not fire until it had been dried carefully and reloaded. The more Fargo considered Paul Hancock, the more of a mystery the man became.

But it was a mystery to be solved later. Fifty-foot-high clouds of black smoke gusted toward the stream and through it Fargo saw real danger. The flames greedily devoured anything that grew, feeding the voracious fire.

"Let's ride," Fargo said, mounting his Ovaro and helping Hancock up behind him again. He was glad he had insisted that they soak their clothing. The heat from the approaching flames began to prickle his skin. The water would evaporate fast but might protect them long enough so they could put a few more miles between their backs and the deadly flames.

"I . . . they're so big. I've never seen a fire so big."

"It's turning, following the bank of the stream," Fargo said. They were safe—or as safe as they could be until the prairie fire burned itself out entirely.

"Where are you heading?" Hancock asked.

"Away from the fire. Far away," Fargo said. "Do you have somewhere better to go?"

"I'm not sure, but I think camp is in this direction."

The notion that Hancock was out on the prairie with others like him made Fargo laugh. He knew it was as much release from the strain of getting away from the fire as anything, and he did not want to make fun of Hancock, but the thought of a dozen more dandies like Hancock struck him as funny.

"It's not?" asked Hancock. "I got turned around while I was hunting for buffalo."

"You're asking me where your camp is?" Fargo continued to be amazed at the man's ignorance. Usually, anyone this witless died fast on the frontier.

"Can you find it? There are ten or so of us. Two wagons, quite a few horses. I remember looking up this morning and seeing twin peaks like those in the distance."

"To the north?"

"I suppose," Hancock said, obviously not sure of directions. "Yes, that way. Those are definitely the hills I saw."

"What brings you out to Wyoming?" Fargo asked. He held the Ovaro to a slow walk to conserve the horse's strength. The fire was burning along the stream, giving them a significant margin of safety now, but he wasn't one to take needless risks.

"Hunting," Hancock said. "For buffalo."

"You're a buffalo hunter? You don't look much like one." Fargo laughed and added, "You don't smell much like one, either. Usually, I have to ride upwind to even get near them after only a day or two of serious shooting."

"Because I bathe is no reason to mock me," Hancock said stiffly.

"I wasn't twitting you. I was only observing that you didn't smell bad." Fargo kept it to himself that Hancock smelled like a whore all dabbed up with cheap French perfume.

"I apologize for being so testy," Hancock said quickly. "This entire ordeal has agitated me."

"Fire will do that," Fargo agreed.

"My horse," Hancock said. "You shot my horse."

"Look," Fargo said, growing exasperated with the man's attitude. "You were all shook up because your horse threw you. I would have let you shoot your own horse if you'd been up to it, but the fire was getting mighty hot."

"Shoot it! Why kill a perfectly good horse?"

"It broke its leg. It was the only merciful thing to do, unless you know some way of putting a splint on a horse's foreleg. I don't."

"That was an expensive horse," Hancock grumbled.

Fargo was at a loss to understand what was going on. Before he could figure out how to ask without raising the prickly man's ire, Hancock bounced up and down and pointed.

"There! There's the camp."

Fargo could hardly believe his eyes as they followed the game trail around a hill into a hollow. Two wagons were parked off to one side, but what wagons! They gleamed in the sun like the finest mahogany bar he had ever seen. Getting closer, Fargo saw the wagons *were* made of mahogany. But the men in the camp were even more of a puzzle.

They dressed in fancy duds, one decked out like a butler in a gray cutaway coat. His white shirt had been boiled and starched so it was as stiff as the man's spine. Stepping forward as if walking barefoot on broken glass, the man looked at Fargo as if he had bitten into a sour persimmon.

"Good morning, sir." His sharp black eyes fixed on Fargo.

"Reckon you're where you belong," Fargo said, looking over the camp and its pristine equipment. Everything he saw was new and expensive.

"Thanks," Hancock said, jumping down clumsily. "Why don't you stay for a bite to eat? It's the least we can do for you."

"Sir," the liveried man said, looking even more disgusted. "I am not sure Mr. Compton would approve. After all, this . . . person . . . is wearing the skin of a dead animal."

Fargo looked at his buckskins. They had been new at the beginning of spring, and he had only worn them for a few months. He knew better than to argue the point. These were strange folks with strange ways, and he wanted nothing to do with them.

"That's all right, Hancock," Fargo said. "Steer clear of that fire and you'll be fine."

"Thanks, Fargo. I appreciate what you've done for me." With that Hancock turned and ignored Fargo.

Fargo turned his Ovaro's face and started for the mountains to the north, away from the flames. When the fire burned itself out it would leave no forage for his horse. Worse than that, it would have driven any buffalo ahead of it, forcing him to run them down. Better to find another herd that hadn't been frightened off by fire.

Fargo had ridden only ten minutes when he heard a horse's hooves pounding hard behind him. He turned and saw a frantic Paul Hancock riding for him, shouting incoherently.

Not sure what the problem was, Fargo reined in and waited for the man to catch up.

"Fargo! Fargo! You've got to help! My sister! She's back there!"

"Back where? In camp?"

"No, no, Melissa is out on the range. In the fire! She's in front of the fire! Help me find her before it's too late!"

2

"Was she alone?" Fargo asked, still wondering what made Hancock tick. It sounded as if his sister was as crazy as he was.

"Yes, she went looking for me but must have gotten turned around, or maybe I told her I was going west and I got confused. It doesn't matter. Mr. Compton said she left right after I did—and she went that way!" Hancock pointed across the stream that had given him and Fargo safe passage to the camp.

"There's no way we can get in front of the fire, if she's there," Fargo said, his lake-blue eyes taking in the details of the wind, the billowing smoke in the distance and the voracious flames still gobbling away at the grass. To venture back into that inferno was crazy. He stroked his beard thoughtfully as he considered what was possible and what wasn't.

"I've got to find her! She'll die out there!"

"Hold your horses," Fargo said, reaching out and grabbing Hancock's arm when the man started to ride toward the raging fire. "You run off without coming up with a plan, and you'll be dead within the hour." He looked at the thick, oily clouds of choking smoke and knew it would not take Hancock that long to find a way to die. "Did this Compton you mentioned see her leave camp?"

"She rode that way," Hancock said, pointing.

"She would have hit the river but wouldn't have gone to the other side," Fargo said, thinking hard. He assumed Melissa Hancock was as maladroit a plainsman as her brother and had similar tastes in clothing. She would not have crossed the stream unless there was a way to avoid getting her fancy duds wet.

"Not unless she found a quick way across," Hancock said, confirming what Fargo suspected. "She was wearing a new riding skirt and a silk blouse. Staining it would be the last thing she'd want to do."

"Of course," Fargo said sarcastically. He turned from his path northward and headed west.

"Wait, Fargo. Are you going to help hunt for her?"

"I'll find her. You get on back to camp and wait there."

"No! Melissa's my sister. I insist on helping to find her."

Fargo saw how scared Hancock was for his sister's safety. While the Trailsman worked better alone, he knew what Hancock felt. He nodded brusquely and set off at a fast pace for the stream. Fargo tried to picture the contours of the land and the way everything sloped to the river. He came to a small rise, saw how the fire burned more to the southwest now, away from the creek.

He could continue along the stream but knew Melissa would have reached the water back in the direction the prairie fire had come from. The Ovaro snorted and shook its head when Fargo insisted on riding parallel to the stream, going toward the plains where the fire had already scorched every living thing.

"Fargo, I—"

Fargo waved Hancock to silence. He had to concentrate as he rode. Finding the woman's trail might not be difficult because she wouldn't have tried to hide it, but the fire changed everything drastically. The grass on this side of the stream was scorched in places, but not burned as it was on the far side. The browned vegetation might conceal even a fresh hoofprint.

After fifteen minutes, Fargo jumped to the ground, knelt, and then laid flat on his belly so he could see the way the dirt had been kicked up near the bank of the stream. He pushed back to his feet and brushed himself off.

"She crossed here," he said. "From the look of it, she

11

was in front of the fire." Fargo knew it did not look good for the woman's survival. She must have been as oblivious to the fire overtaking her as her brother had been earlier.

"Then she's all right. Melissa is a good horsewoman. She could outrun the fire," Hancock said.

"It might have happened that way," Fargo allowed, although he doubted it. He climbed back on the paint and started across the stream. It was shallow here, which might have been the reason Melissa chose to cross. She could ride without getting too wet since the stream rose only halfway to the Ovaro's belly.

On the other side, the grass was burned level to the ground, leaving behind only crumbly black ash. All trace of Melissa's tracks were gone, burned clean away. Fargo hesitated to continue riding in a straight line since that would bring them up to the rear of the prairie fire. The ground was still hot and presented danger to their horses. He did not cotton much to giving the Ovaro a hot foot.

"She got away, didn't she?" asked Hancock. For the first time, he sounded as if it finally occurred to him what it meant for his sister to have crossed in front of the fire.

"We'll find her," vowed Fargo, but he did not want to promise that he would find the woman alive.

They rode in silence, Fargo guiding them more on instinct than visible tracks. He let the Ovaro follow the contours of the land, taking the easy path wherever possible because he thought Melissa would have given her own horse its head. They soon topped a rise looking out over the sizzling line of burning grass a mile away. The wind had died down, but the fire refused to go out, choosing only to drift slowly across the basin.

"See that spot?" asked Fargo, staring at a rocky area that had somehow avoided the ravages of the capricious fire. "Your sister might have taken refuge there."

"If she knew the fire was coming," Hancock said, dejected. The man rode slumped in the saddle, as if he expected to find Melissa's body at every turn.

"She knew," Fargo said with assurance. "She couldn't have missed it because she was dead in front of it." He immediately regretted the way he phrased that. Hancock jerked as if he had been poked in the gut when Fargo uttered the word "dead."

"If she didn't notice, her horse would have," Fargo went on, hoping to keep Hancock occupied with hunting for the lost woman. It didn't pay to linger on possibilities when they didn't know what had happened. Yet.

"Fargo, look! See that patch of red? That's Melissa's blouse!" Hancock exclaimed. He spurred his horse forward before Fargo could stop him.

Again Hancock rode through the land oblivious to all that went on around him. Fargo saw that the wind had died, letting the fire move only by slow gnawing at the unburned grass. But now the wind was shifting direction and began whipping up tall flames again—turning the fire at a new angle that would intercept anyone riding straight for the rocky tract.

"Stop!" Fargo shouted, but Hancock couldn't hear him over the pounding of his horse's hooves. The fire picked up speed and moved to cut Hancock off. There wasn't much dried grass left to fuel it, but enough remained to make the fire deadly.

Fargo tried to follow but was too slow. The heat from the blaze forced him to curve away from the route Hancock had taken. A thousand different plans flashed through Fargo's head. When he saw a break in the fire that would let him get through to the rocky area where Hancock had spotted his sister's blouse, he took it.

Smoke and fire rearing around him, Fargo shot through the notch and felt his beard begin to smolder. He swatted at it, got his head down and let the Ovaro lead the way. The horse would take him through faster by picking its own way than if Fargo guessed at where safe passage lay in the roiling clouds of eye-biting smoke.

Less than a minute after being engulfed by smoke and fire, Fargo popped out into a relatively clear area. The fire stretched behind him, cutting off escape toward the stream. But ahead lay the rocky region and the bright crimson flag fluttering from a charred bush that Hancock had seen.

Fargo looked all around for Paul Hancock but couldn't find him. The thick haze of choking smoke blanketing the basin cut off sight in all directions save straight ahead. Fargo rode like his life depended on it—and it did.

The paint's hooves clattered on stone and signaled that he had reached relative safety. What sparse vegetation had been here was already burned away. Fargo cut across the rocky stretch and got to the twig where a streamer of red silk fluttered. Melissa had come this way and had lost much of her blouse sleeve. He grabbed at the cloth and examined it, then looked around.

There was only one direction the woman could have gone after losing her entire sleeve to the thorny bush. Fargo went that way and was relieved to feel the heat slacken as he rode deeper into the rocky terrain. The sudden downslope took him by surprise as a small gully turned into a minor canyon. From a distance he would never have known this existed.

His heart beat a little faster when he saw the rest of the red silk blouse—and the woman wearing it.

Fargo galloped forward and dismounted on the run to reach Melissa Hancock's side. She lay sprawled facedown on the ground. He saw no trace of her horse and guessed it must have thrown her. A gash just above her right eyebrow showed where she had collided hard with the ground as she went flying.

"Wh-what's happening?" she moaned. She reached up feebly to touch the cut. She jerked her hand away when her fingers found only blood. The dark-haired woman's eyelids fluttered and then eyes as blue as Fargo's own stared up. "Who are you?" she asked.

"Your brother sent me to find you."

"Where's Paul?" She struggled to sit up, but Fargo saw her strength had yet to return.

"You took quite a knock on the head. Let me help you up."

"My horse reared," she said. "I remember that. A snake?"

"The fire," Fargo said.

14

"Yes, that was it. The fire. All around me, so fast. It was like a bad dream."

It seemed that way to Fargo, also, except he knew the stark reality of the flames. The rocky hollow gave some protection, but the air was getting thick with smoke. If the fire continued to burn all around, they might not be able to breathe much longer without choking.

"Do you know what happened to your horse?" he asked Melissa.

"I . . . I don't remember that. Gone," she said weakly. Melissa started to take a step away from Fargo, but her legs gave out. He caught her before she collapsed to the ground. Taking the woman in his arms might have been enjoyable under other circumstances. Now all he could think of was getting away from the fire filling the deep ravine with black smoke.

Fargo unceremoniously tossed her belly-down over the saddle, let the Ovaro become accustomed to the weight, then mounted himself. He shifted Melissa's weight a little; then it cantered the horse along the gully as he hunted for a way out. Going back the way he had come was out of the question. He could see the smoke boiling down the slope as if it had a noxious life of its own. Where the fire found enough grass and other vegetation to produce so much smoke he didn't know and he certainly wasn't inclined to find out.

The Ovaro picked its way along the rocky floor, then struggled up a steeper slope a half mile along from where Fargo had found the woman. Fargo found himself looking down at Melissa Hancock, wondering what brought her and her brother to the frontier. He couldn't help noticing that her hands were free of calluses and her face was as of yet unweathered by sun or wind. She was city-bred, from the look of her, and Fargo was doing plenty of looking.

He had seen prettier women in his day, but not too many. And none of them had been draped over his saddle in front of him so their pert behinds stuck up in the air. Melissa's long hair dangled down precariously, but Fargo could not pull her up far enough to keep it from tangling in vegetation.

Let it get dirty, he thought. *She can wash it later. When she's safe.*

The longer he rode the more secure Fargo felt that they would be safe from the fire. The perverse wind had died again, leaving the heavy pall of smoke in the ravine—but no new smoke sank down like the suffocating blanket that he had narrowly escaped prior. Soon enough, the paint got to the top of the slope and Fargo sucked in a deep breath of fresh air.

Fargo halted and looked around, saw a path through burned grass toward the stream and decided not to wait for Melissa to come to before heading for the water. He needed to get the soot off his face and a long, cool drink appealed mightily to him. The journey across the smoldering land was a nightmare, but Fargo made good time in spite of watering eyes and a heavy cough caused by the clinging smoke.

Melissa Hancock stirred as he made his way across the stream to the unburned side. The water splashing up on her brought her back to a groggy consciousness that caused her to thrash about and sputter.

Fargo put his hand on her back, got his leg up and over, then slid to the ground in time to catch her as she flopped off. He held her in his arms, easing her to the ground.

"Let me get some water for you," he said. He grabbed his canteen, emptied the stale water and refilled it with the water from the stream. Then he soaked his bandanna before returning.

Melissa sat staring into the distance, as if still stunned. He put the wet bandanna on her forehead and handed her the canteen.

"Drink," he said. "You need it."

"Who are you?" she asked, looking up at him with her bright eyes.

"You're welcome," Fargo said dryly.

"I'm sorry," Melissa said, wiping the grime off her face and then taking a long pull from the canteen. She choked, wiped her lips, and tried again with better luck. "I don't know happened. I went looking for my brother, and the fire just came up. I don't know where it came from."

"Prairie fires move fast," Fargo said, trying to ease her mind. He thought she was a fool for going out without knowing what was happening all around, but he had seen that she, like her brother, was a rank greenhorn.

"Paul!" she exclaimed, trying to get to her feet.

"Take it easy," Fargo said. "Paul rode out of your camp with me, but we got separated. He's probably back at the wagons waiting for you."

"He tried to rescue me?" The notion struck the dark-haired woman as funny. Or it might have been a nervous release since she realized how close she had come to dying. Melissa laughed until tears ran down her cheeks, leaving sooty tracks wherever they touched. She dabbed at them with the damp bandanna and got herself under control.

"It's a ways back to your camp. We'd better get moving."

"The fire?" Melissa said, fear causing her eyes to go wide.

"It's burned itself out," Fargo said. "All that's left are embers. I just want to get you home before sundown."

"It's hard to tell what time it is," Melissa said, looking around. "The smoke is still so thick."

Fargo helped her onto the Ovaro but remained on the ground to walk alongside. He had a dozen questions to ask about her and her brother, but held his tongue. His curiosity would be satisfied sooner or later. It took the better part of two hours to return to the camp with its fancy-dressed servants. They got into camp as the sun dipped low in the west and cast long shadows.

"Ah, my dear, you have returned!" A slight, almost effeminate man rushed out to help Melissa down from the horse. "You gave us quite a fright."

"Where's Paul?" she asked. "Have you seen him, Mr. Compton?"

Fargo studied the man, trying to get a handle on him. Compton was older than he appeared at first, possibly in his late twenties. There wasn't much tribulation burned into his face; he had lived an easy life. He wore store-bought clothes that cost more than Fargo saw in cash in a year—in a good year.

"I thought he would come back with you," Compton said. He eyed Fargo as if he were a new and intriguing museum exhibit. "I see you have found another savior. How are you, my good man? I am Justin Compton." He thrust out his hand for Fargo to shake.

Fargo took the hand and was surprised at the strength he found there. He had expected the firmness of India rubber.

"You must be a local," Compton said.

"The name's Skye Fargo. Glad to be of help. Miss Hancock was in a bad way, but she seems to be in good hands now." He touched the brim of his hat politely and started to mount. There was nothing for him in Justin Compton's camp.

"Wait, Mr. Fargo. Paul's not back. That must mean he is still on the plains. He might be hurt or in terrible danger." Melissa was obviously distraught over the fate of her brother.

"We got cut off after we rode out after you," Fargo explained. "He probably followed the stream and is camping out there, all safe and sound."

From the woman's expression, the notion of her brother camping struck real fear in her heart.

"Please go find him. I can't thank you enough for what you did for me, but Paul—"

"There, there, my dear," soothed Compton, putting his arm around her shoulders. "Mr. Fargo seems a knowledgeable man. If he says Paul is safe, he must be."

Compton's words rankled. Fargo saw the way the man stared at him and knew the dandy was expert at this kind of needling.

"Looking for your brother's trail in the dark is a fool's errand. I can go out at first light."

"Splendid!" cried Compton. "You must dine with us this evening then. My chef has fixed a special meal, antic-ipating Miss Hancock's return."

"Chef?" Fargo looked at Compton, then to Melissa Hancock.

"He means chuck-wagon cook," she said, as if explaining something complex to an idiot child. "Pierre is very good. He certainly does better than beans and bacon."

The cooking odor made Fargo's mouth water. It had been weeks since he had eaten a decent meal. Going after Paul Hancock now that twilight was turning into a completely dark, moonless night was out of the question.

"I'd be right happy to sample some of Pierre's victuals," Fargo said. This produced the reaction he expected. Compton clapped his hands with delight at having found a genuine Wild West aborigine, and Melissa gave a sigh of relief that Fargo would track down her brother.

Fargo wondered if he had anything to be happy about, other than a full belly and a good night's sleep.

3

Fargo stretched tired muscles and yawned as he sat up in his bedroll. It was still a half hour before dawn painted the eastern sky with pinks and grays. He wanted to be out of the camp on Paul Hancock's trail at first light so he began assembling his gear, readying for the hunt.

He jerked around at the sound of soft footsteps behind him. Fargo kept his hand away from his Colt and was glad when he saw Justin Compton. The man was dressed in bizarre fringed clothing that parodied Fargo's own worn buckskins. But Compton dressed in fancy cloth rather than tough, durable deer hide. In his hands he held a large-bore rifle, as if he intended to use it as a club rather than a firearm.

"It's a .60-caliber Hawken rifle," Compton said when he saw Fargo's interest. "Designed to bring down the fiercest of buffalos."

"Is that what brings you to Wyoming?" Fargo asked as he finished tying up his bedroll. There was a moment's hesitation before Compton answered, making Fargo wonder if the man might be lying. Or not telling the complete truth.

"I want to bag one of the woollies," Compton said. "Hunting is great sport, you see, Mr. Fargo. I take it quite seriously."

"That has the look of a serious rifle," Fargo allowed. He heaved his saddle up and onto his shoulder so he could leave. His Ovaro was corralled with the rest of Compton's horses.

"I want to go with you, sir."

"What?" This stopped Fargo dead in his tracks. Letting Hancock accompany him to hunt for his sister the day before had been a mistake, but one Fargo would, make again. A man's duty to family ought to be paramount, and he would have thought less of Hancock if the young man had not insisted. But there wasn't any reason he could think of that explained Compton's interest in finding Paul Hancock.

"I hired him. I am responsible for him."

"What does Hancock do for you?" Fargo turned and headed for the corral. He had thought he was beyond surprise, but he was wrong. Compton's outrageous answer stopped him in his tracks again.

"He's my scout. A guide through these terrible, desolate lands."

"Paul Hancock is leading your hunting expedition?" Fargo fought to keep from laughing in the man's face. If everything Hancock knew about the frontier was stuffed into a thimble there would still be room for a buffalo or two.

"He has done well getting me to these grassy plains. We found spoor from buffalo at every turn, but the fire explains why we have not found any in the flesh."

"The fire drove them off," Fargo guessed. He heaved his saddle onto the Ovaro's back and went about the chore of cinching it down for what might be a long day's ride.

"I am sure that is what happened," Compton said without any guile. He snapped his fingers as if this would make everything right. To Fargo's amusement, it almost worked that way. The snooty butler led a saddled horse from the far side of the corral for Compton. The man easily climbed into the saddle, settled himself, and rested the long-barreled rifle in the crook of his left arm.

"You don't have to come along," Fargo said. "I'll have Hancock back before nightfall or know the reason."

"The reason might be that he has perished," Compton said. He sniffed delicately, took a linen handkerchief from his pocket and dabbed at his nose, then tucked it away. "I know the dangers, sir. I have lived at the edge of civilization enough to know that Mr. Hancock might have died in the fire. If so, you will want a witness, some-one to help dig the grave, someone to vouch for you."

"Vouch for me?"

"Isn't that necessary?" asked Compton. "When a man is discovered dead, aren't the authorities likely to question how it happened?"

"What authorities?" asked Fargo. He looked around Thunder Basin. The stench from the fire lingered. It was sixty miles or more to Caspar and perhaps thirty to New-castle. The notion that a marshal or even a sheriff might be out on the grasslands patrolling, looking for outlaws who might commit a crime or someone who had hap-pened on a corpse, was crazy. The land was too big and the lawmen too few for that to be much of a worry.

"This is a rather isolated portion of the countryside, isn't it?" Compton said, as if only coming to that fact slowly. "All the more reason for us to ride together. Should anything happen to you, I shall be able to rescue you."

"Stay in camp with Miss Hancock," Fargo said. "I'll be back as fast as I can." He put his heels to the Ovaro's flanks and shot out of the corral. Compton followed, quickly catching up with Fargo and riding at his shoulder.

"I have an obligation to Mr. Hancock that I cannot allow another to discharge." Compton laughed and held up his heavy rifle. "Besides, I might get a chance to discharge *this*!"

Fargo ignored the man and settled down to ride for the last spot he had seen Paul Hancock. By the time he reached the spot where the fire had separated them, dawn gave enough light for him to find Hancock's tracks. In places the fire had baked the tracks into a permanent trail as if the indentations had been turned to pottery. But Fargo's skills were put to the test quickly when the scorched area became so severe no hope of spotting a hoofprint remained.

All the while Fargo had hunted for Hancock's trail, Compton had kept silent. Now he let out a whoop of glee, stood in his stirrups and pointed.

"There, Mr. Fargo! Buffalos!"

"Stop that," Fargo said, reaching to grab the long barrel of the rifle as Compton lifted it to his shoulder. "You can't shoot from horseback."

"I need something to steady the rifle," Compton said, seeing the problem as his horse began hopping around. He got it under control, dropped the rifle back to its resting spot in the cradle of his left arm, and shielded his eyes against the morning sun. "An entire herd. We can feast tonight if I bag one of those monsters."

"What about finding Hancock?" asked Fargo.

"He'll turn up. This is my chance to get a fine buffalo-skin robe. And a steak! Pierre will prove his mastery of the culinary arts this evening!"

Fargo started to tell Compton to be careful not to stampede the herd. There were ways to cut out a solitary buffalo and shoot it without spooking the rest, but Compton was already galloping toward the herd intent on his trophy.

Fargo reluctantly followed, knowing Compton could get himself into more trouble in a hurry. He intended to get back onto Hancock's trail, but having the buffalos thundering across the basin limited where he could search. If Compton was not careful, the buffalos might trample the ground so much that Fargo could never find Hancock's tracks.

"An entire herd," chortled Compton as he dismounted. He pulled out a tripod for his rifle and drove it into the scorched ground. Dropping the heavy barrel into the U atop the tripod, he sighted in on a powerful bull buffalo half a mile away. Fargo or any competent buffalo hunter could make the shot at this distance, but he doubted Compton would do more than scare the herd.

"Don't take that one," Fargo called to the hunter. "Bulls are tough eating. Pick a smaller one, a cow."

"This one has horns big enough to fill the wall in my study back in New York," Compton said, wiggling around as he squinted down the sights to shoot.

Fargo judged the windage and decided that was not a factor this morning. The winds the day before that had whipped the fire across this land had died along with

23

most of the vegetation. The buffalos were making good progress across the burned region on their way to greener pastures untouched by fire. He estimated the herd at two or three hundred, a small one considering there were more than ten million buffalos on this side of the Mississippi.

His eyes went from the brown, shaggy, woolly hides to the path they followed. Fargo went cold inside when he spotted a man waving frantically from in front of the herd.

"Compton, don't shoot!" Fargo barked. He galloped off to get in front of the herd—and to rescue Paul Hancock.

Fargo heard Compton's rifle hammer fall on a punk round. The hissing, spitting sound was immediately followed by Compton's voluble curses, and a metallic grinding as the cartridge ejected and a new one was slammed in. He had no time to stop Compton. The man had to see what was happening and not shoot.

He had to or Hancock would be trampled. As fast as Fargo galloped, there might be two of them kicked and stamped to death by the buffalos.

"Fargo, here, my horse! It died. I'm on foot."

Fargo kept his head down as he raced along the burned prairie toward Hancock. He didn't want to know what had happened to Hancock's second horse. The man was jinxed and should never be allowed astride another animal again. But he realized his danger and came toward Fargo, his gait a combination of a fast walk and a run. Fargo wished Hancock would stay still and not act as a distraction for the lead buffalo. The shaggy beasts were like bulls. Unexpected motion in front of them caused extreme anger, and they charged.

The horns Compton coveted so much were not only ornamental. Fargo had seen them gut a man with a single toss powered by a buffalo's strong neck muscles.

As Fargo reached Hancock, he heard the sharp crack of Compton's rifle. Fargo raced past a frantic Paul Hancock, reached down and grabbed his arm, jerking him aloft. Hancock almost bounced off the Ovaro's rump, then got his balance enough to scoot forward behind Fargo.

"The herd," Hancock gasped out.

"I know. Your boss shot at a buffalo and spooked them all."

- The ground began to shake. Fargo had the image of being on an Indian's drum head. At first there were only a few vibrations, then as the war dance grew faster, the pounding on the drum made anything on the head bounce around.

"The noise," shouted Hancock. "I can't hear anything else."

Fargo didn't bother answering. He would have had to shout over the thundering hooves of the entire stampeding herd. Riding back the way he had come would ensure their deaths because the flank of the herd closest to Compton had stampeded first. The rest of the herd was slower to respond, but respond they would, with a vengeance until all three hundred of the massive brutes were in full, panic-driven flight.

Fargo angled away, hoping the buffalos would not follow. To his dismay, they turned and came directly after him, as if he were their leader. The Ovaro began to strain under the double weight and impossible speed over the plains. Fargo had the choice of going up a hill or down a small valley that led to the stream some distance off.

He sawed at the reins and got the powerful stallion headed up the gradual slope.

"You'll tire your horse. Go down there. It's all downhill," cried Hancock.

Fargo ignored the advice. He knew something about frightened herds. They followed him now, but if he vanished their leaders would choose an easier path—down the very valley Hancock wanted them to ride.

The Ovaro stumbled, but kept going until they reached the top of the rise. Fargo urged the exhausted horse a bit farther, then cut back sharply once he was out of view of the herd. The fringes of the herd reached the top of the hill, failed to see him because he had already ridden back almost halfway past the herd, then turned and followed the still-panicked leaders toward the stream.

Only then did Fargo draw rein and slump forward. He patted his horse's neck, then slid from the saddle. Hancock joined him on the ground.

"Thanks, Fargo. You pulled my fat out of the fire again. That's twice I owe you my life."

"Three," Fargo said, mopping at his forehead. He got off a caked layer of dust and soot. "You own me three times. I found your sister and returned her to Compton's camp."

"Melissa!" Hancock cried. "She's all right? She wasn't hurt?"

"She got lost. She also got lucky and stumbled into a rocky region where the fire didn't fry her."

"I'm so glad," Hancock said, sinking to the ground. He leaned forward and put his face in his hands. Fargo thought the man was going to cry, but he didn't.

"There you gents are," came Justin Compton's cheery voice. "I bagged it!"

"What's that?" Hancock looked up. Rage replaced shock as he shot to his feet. "You killed a buffalo? You started that stampede when I was in front of the herd? You could have killed me!"

"I say, that's a shoddy attitude, Mr. Hancock. You look hale and hearty to me."

"Thanks to Fargo," Hancock said.

"I knew you would come through for us with flying colors, Mr. Fargo. You have that . . . competent look about you." Compton seemed to hesitate. "Now, about that buffalo I shot—"

"You don't know what to do with it," Fargo finished for him. "I'm sure Hancock can help out. He's your guide, after all."

"Please," muttered Hancock. "I . . . we can use some help dressing out such a large animal. It was a big one, wasn't it, Mr. Compton?"

"Oh, quite large," the dandy said with some pride.

"We'll give you a fair share of the meat and anything else you might want," Hancock said. The forlorn look in his eyes convinced Fargo that one more good deed wouldn't be amiss. He motioned for Hancock to mount so they could return to the kill site.

It took twenty minutes of slow walking to get there, but once they had reached the downed buffalo, Fargo was glad he had agreed to help. It was a sturdy cow, well fleshed and undoubtedly tender eating.

"I've worked up a powerful thirst," Compton said, licking his lips. "I wish I had a bottle of that fine claret of Pierre's."

"If you're thirsty, I have a treat for you. The Sioux claim there's nothing better under the sun to drink, not even firewater," Fargo said. "Get a cup."

"Right here." Compton said, fishing about in his saddlebags for a small silver cup.

Fargo drew his Arkansas toothpick and went to the buffalo. He placed his hand on its belly, then prodded gently until he found the right spot. A quick stab and a long slash opened the cow's belly. Green fluid gushed out. Fargo grabbed the cup from Compton and filled it, then handed it to the man.

"Go on, drink," Fargo said. When he saw Compton staring askance at the bile, Fargo took the cup back and downed the contents in a single gulp. He filled the cup again and savored the juices this time. A third cup he offered to the men.

Hancock hesitantly took it, sipped, then drank it down.

"That's mighty fine," he said, smacking his lips.

"Then I shall have some, also," Compton declared. But he swallowed hard after his cup. It might have been the taste or the way Fargo was butchering the cow.

To the Trailsman it didn't matter. He wanted to get the men back to their camp, take his share of the meat, and be done with them and their airs. He didn't know where he was heading, but as long as it was away from these greenhorns it was fine with him.

4

"We shouldn't leave the carcass out here like this," Fargo said, looking at what remained of the buffalo. He had butchered it the best he could, but his and Compton's horses could not take more than they had slung over their haunches. As it was, they would have to walk back to camp.

"There's nothing more I need," Compton said airily. He sniffed delicately at the rising odor from the dead animal, then turned and put his hand on the buffalo hide. He stroked over it like he might touch a lover's cheek.

At that thought, Fargo tensed. Somehow, he could not see Compton and Melissa Hancock together, but there had to be a reason that Justin Compton had hired her and her brother as "guides." Even a tenderfoot like Compton had to see right away how inept the Hancocks were.

"We can get back to your camp before nightfall," Fargo said, judging how far they had ridden and the terrain separating them from the fancy wagons and Compton's French chef.

"Then let us trek on!" Compton said with gusto. Head high and whistling a tune Fargo did not recognize, Compton set off in the direction of his small expedition.

Hancock and Fargo trailed. Fargo saw Hancock wanted to explain about his boss, but Fargo never gave him the chance. What went on between the Hancocks and their employer was none of his business. Fargo was content to think about riding on alone, letting the beautiful country swallow him up. It wouldn't take more than a day's ride to get out of the burned area and into mountains where he could breathe fresh air and drink pure water from the streams.

"He, uh, he's not entirely what he appears," Hancock said. "Mr. Compton, I mean."

"He must be a good hunter," Fargo said. "He brought down a buffalo at more than a quarter mile with a single shot." He didn't know whether to attribute it to marksmanship or pure luck, but it didn't hurt to give Compton the benefit of the doubt. After all, he was never going to see him or the rest of his company again.

"He's good at a lot of strange things. He is quite the artist. I've never seen anyone better able to capture the beauty of everything around us with a few quick pencil strokes. Mr. Compton has a dozen notebooks filled with sketches and numbers and even pressed leaves and particles of rock."

"Numbers?" asked Fargo.

"I don't know what they mean. I asked once when we were outside of Leavenworth, but he gave me a flippant answer. But the drawings are quite remarkable. I think he means to sell them to art dealers back in New York after he returns home."

"Is that where he gets his money? He must be really rich to outfit wagons as ornate as those and to bring along a personal cook." Fargo did not bother adding how Compton wasted his money on the likes of Paul and Melissa. They must be nothing more than window dressing for the man, a couple that looked nice alongside him as he rode.

"I'm not sure where his money comes from. His father, I suspect. Melissa said something about a remark Mr. Compton made concerning working for his family's company, but she never got it straight what he really meant."

"A man of mystery," Fargo observed. He stared at the back of Compton's head as the man strutted along. The way Compton walked displayed great arrogance and assurance of command, but Fargo saw the tiny jerks of his head, the way his eyes fixed on something out on Thunder Basin, following flights of birds aloft. Compton tried to seem above such natural things but secretly took it all in.

"There's our camp," Hancock said, heaving a sigh of relief. "My feet are killing me. I never thought I'd get used to riding all day, but walking!"

Fargo looked at him from the corner of his eye. This reinforced his belief that Hancock was a city dweller and unused to the frontier, no matter what claim Justin Compton might make to the contrary about hiring Paul as a guide. But Fargo's attention focused more firmly on Hancock's sister. Melissa was cleaned up now and wore elegant clothing. Even in his occasional trips to St. Louis to sell his beaver pelts and other furs Fargo had never seen a woman better dressed.

Her long, raven hair had been washed and now cascaded past her shoulders. The evening breeze tugged lightly and caused it to ripple like a banner. Her lovely oval face, the swell of her breasts, delightfully trim waist, and womanly hips all drew Fargo.

"How do you like it?" Melissa asked. Fargo was not sure who she spoke to as she pirouetted to show off the form-clinging white blouse, her long brown velvet skirt, and the expensive Spanish leather shoes beneath.

"You are a vision of loveliness, my dear," Compton exclaimed. "For you and you alone I dedicate this, my first kill of the safari."

"A buffalo?" she asked.

Compton answered at length, but Fargo saw Melissa's bright sapphire eyes were fixed on him. She knew what the shaggy pelt was and only wanted to keep Compton occupied.

He smiled at her and got one in return, but it was not enough for Fargo to want to remain with the Compton party one second longer than necessary.

"Bruno, Charles, come unpack all this wonderful meat and get it to Pierre right away. Hurry now," ordered Compton, clapping his hands as two servants hurried up to obey.

"Will you stay, Mr. Fargo? For dinner?" asked Melissa. Her bold gaze never wavered. Neither did Fargo's determination to leave. He saw the dark-haired woman's brother stiffen a little as he realized what was passing between the two. Fargo had no idea of Melissa and Justin Compton's relationship. To step into the middle of that would be worse than walking barefoot through a den of rattlers.

"Tell your cook to fix you a section of the intestine," Fargo said. "Boil it until it's white and hardly more than a paste. You might like it."

"Then you won't be staying?" asked Paul Hancock, stepping between Fargo and his sister. "That's a shame. You've saved my life—and Melissa's. We owe you a true debt of gratitude."

"Yes, he's right, of course," Compton spoke up, again drawing attention to himself. "I owe you for your help in bagging this noble creature." Compton stroked over the buffalo hide and almost purred like a kitten with a bowl of cream. He pulled his hand away reluctantly. "I have great plans for this," he said. "And I am sure you have travel plans of your own, sir. I wish you a speedy trip to wherever it is you drift so aimlessly."

"Thanks," Fargo said dryly, knowing a dismissal when he heard one. He tipped his hat in Melissa's direction and saw her look of dejection. He felt a pang himself but knew better than to change his mind.

Fargo swung into the saddle and rode from Compton's camp without so much as a look back. The sun was dipping low in the west, but Fargo headed that way nonetheless. Pulling down the brim of his floppy hat helped keep the bright light from his eyes but did nothing to stop the feeling that he was wrong not to stay with Compton's party. They were like babes in the woods and had no idea what they faced as they blundered out among the wild animals. So far they had all been lucky, but with or without Fargo's help, that luck would run out eventually.

He hoped Melissa was spared from whatever the future held, be it fire or buffalo stampede or simple starvation. No one in the band had enough experience on the frontier to avoid even simple accidents.

Fargo kept riding, though. He could not wet-nurse them until they returned to New York. It wasn't his job, and he shouldn't have felt even a small tug of obligation. Yet he did.

That night he camped by a small brook spilling from the highlands ahead. He stretched out his bedroll and lay staring up at the stars, making odd patterns of them and wondering if the future was indeed written there, as some Indian shamans claimed. By the time his eyelids began to droop, he had decided it wasn't his destiny to know—or even care. Live one day at a time and enjoy what he could, change what he didn't like, and if he couldn't enjoy it or change it, then move on.

As he slipped into deeper sleep, strange noises filled the night. A sudden drumbeat brought Fargo straight up, his hand clutching his six-shooter. His heart raced as he looked around, fearing he was about to be ambushed by Sioux. Familiar nighttime sounds nearby assured him he was safe enough for the moment.

The distant drums spelled trouble eventually, however. Fargo had heard that rhythmic beat before and knew its full meaning. The Sioux were on the warpath and danced through the night to whip themselves into a killing frenzy.

Fargo hastily gathered his gear and fastened it behind his saddle, then mounted.

"Sorry," he said to his paint, "but I have to know what's brewing." The horse reluctantly headed out. Fargo kept it at a slow walk to keep from suffering the same fate as Paul Hancock's horse. He was sure the paint was more surefooted, and plunging blindly through the darkness was something he would never do, unless it was a matter of life and death.

Fargo sucked in a deep breath and held it for a moment. The powerful drumbeat hinted that this might be such a matter.

For an hour Fargo rode, getting closer to the drums. He distinguished between four different drummers now, each using a subtly distinct beat. If four drummed that meant as many as four hundred warriors might be dancing. This posed a major threat throughout eastern Wyoming from the Sioux.

Bonfires lit the meadow as Fargo rounded a small hill and saw hundreds of tepees. Dark figures moved sinuously around the fires. At this distance Fargo could not make out details but knew the Sioux were decked out in war paint and brandished knives and war clubs. He dismounted and tethered his Ovaro to a stunted mountain ash tree, so he could scout ahead on foot.

With so many Sioux occupied with their war dance he did not expect to find many sentries, especially a quarter mile from the temporary village. Only his quick reflexes and long experience saved him when he discovered how wrong he was.

A moccasin scuffling along the grass was his only warning to take cover. Fargo fell facedown and lay still beside a rotting log as the Sioux brave walked past slowly. The Indian carried a rifle and had two knives thrust into his broad hide belt. Fargo couldn't tell for sure but thought the brave might also have a six-gun.

The Sioux warrior stopped three feet from Fargo looked around curiously, sniffed the air, and spun in a full circle. As the sentry turned his back, Fargo found himself confronted with a choice: lie still and trust that the brave did not spot him or attack and remove the threat. Permanently.

Fargo was under no illusion that he could simply knock out the Indian. War paint gleamed in the faint starlight and every move the man made told of readiness to kill. Besides, leaving a sentry unconscious or even tied and gagged while he went into the village was a prescription for disaster if another sentry came by.

Fargo imitated the log beside him as the Sioux turned back, almost facing in Fargo's direction. Then the Indian walked past, almost stepping on him. The soft whisper of moccasins faded as the guard continued to protect his village.

Only when he was certain the lookout had gone into a small stand of white birch did Fargo move. Quieter than the Indian, he made his way toward the village to get a better idea what was going on. Twice more he slipped past pickets until he was within a hundred yards of a large fire where scores of braves danced wildly.

Settling down, Fargo watched carefully as the chiefs and subchiefs moved through the lines of dancers, talking and sometimes going off by themselves. His heart raced when he spotted a group of four, two decked out in eagle-feather war bonnets showing their exalted position among warriors, and the other two sporting long strings of scalps from their belts. They were up-and-coming subchiefs from their look.

The four began talking in low tones that grew more strident. Fargo caught words now and then, enough to know that Wyoming was likely to be the scene of a major uprising soon. He didn't understand enough of the rapid-fire Sioux lingo to be certain, but the tribal leaders were upset with the way white miners were moving into the Badlands, hunting relentlessly for gold. He got the sense that something more had sparked this rebellion, over and above the intrusion of the metal-hungry miners.

Fargo took a deep breath to settle his racing pulse when he heard that this large village made up only half of the war party. Almost two thousand Sioux were on the warpath.

Something had riled the Indians, and it wasn't likely to end any way but in blood.

"Compton," Fargo muttered under his breath. The foolish rich man would blunder directly into the path of the Sioux and end up with his scalp dangling from a brave's belt. The fate for a beautiful woman like Melissa Hancock would be even more brutal. If she was lucky, she would die when the Sioux attacked.

If she wasn't lucky, she would be taken alive to be a slave.

With the drums pounding and the electricity created by so many kill-crazy Sioux filling the air, Fargo slipped into the darkness and headed back to where he had tethered his horse. He avoided two lookouts with no trouble and was ready to mount when the Ovaro shied.

Fargo knew better than to ignore the horse's reaction to him climbing into the saddle. Throwing hismelf to one side saved his life. An arrow thwacked into the saddle about where his head had been an instant before. The stallion reared and began pawing the air.

The arrow that had almost taken his life had come from behind. He rolled and came to his knees, the long blade of the Arkansas toothpick pointed directly into the shadows that billowed, grew, and then exploded in size. A burly Sioux warrior rushed out, bow and arrow abandoned in favor of a war club swung high over his head. He bowled Fargo over, but Fargo was ready for the attack and grabbed the front of the brave's jerkin and kicked and twisted hard as he thrust upward with his knife.

A rush of wetness engulfed Fargo's hand as the Indian went limp. Fargo pushed him to the ground, rolled him over, and pulled his knife from the man's chest. The blade had spread two ribs and let the sharp tip puncture the warrior's heart.

Fargo ran his bloody hand through tufts of grass beside the body, then wiped off his knife blade before resheathing it. He touched his forehead, glad he still had a scalp where it belonged. Fargo sat back on his heels and listened hard for any sound in the night that might give away other Sioux braves near him.

The pounding war drums beat more frantically and war chants rose to challenge the night.

Fargo looped rope around the dead man's ankles, fastened the other end to his pommel, then gently put his heels to the Ovaro's flanks and got the horse moving through the night. For over a mile Fargo dragged the body until he found a deep ravine.

Here he dug a shallow grave and laid the warrior to rest. A few rocks atop the mound would keep coyotes and wolves from digging up the grave's contents for a while. Fargo hoped it would keep the Sioux from going out scouting for the missing sentry. Without a body, the Indians would never be certain what had happened.

Dusting off his hands, Fargo climbed once more into the saddle and headed back to Compton's camp to warn them of the uprising.

5

Fargo had no trouble finding Compton and his pair of mahogany-and-brass wagons. They left a trail a blind man could follow as they pushed on across the burned basin toward the north. He thanked his lucky stars that Compton had not chosen to follow the buffalo herd to make another kill. That would have led his party directly into the arms of the Sioux war party.

"Hallo!" cried Paul Hancock from the back of the second wagon. He waved to Fargo and beckoned him on. Fargo picked up his pace and trotted after the wagons, reaching Hancock within a few minutes of the man spotting him.

"I hadn't expected to see you again, Fargo," said Hancock. His greeting carried a mixture of antagonism and wistfulness. Fargo reckoned the man didn't want him meddling with whatever deal he had going with Justin Compton, but also wanted someone who could provide some solid experience to counter his own ignorance of trail lore.

"Where's Compton? You've got troubles—big troubles."

"What's wrong?" asked Hancock, his hand going to a holstered six-shooter. Fargo was not happy to see the brand-new Smith & Wesson still at Paul's side. He doubted Hancock was any better a shot than he was a frontiersman.

"There's no need to tell it twice. Let's find Compton so I can tell you all at the same time." Fargo was in no mood to bandy words and worried that Hancock might try to argue with him about the Indian trouble brewing.

Fargo trotted to the front wagon and convinced the

driver, Charles, to stop. Compton and Melissa were in the back of the wagon poring over a map as if they were sitting in a parlor.

"Skye," Melissa said, her smile warm and bright enough to rival the sun. "You're back."

"Mr. Compton, you've got to turn back east and get out of Wyoming as fast as you can."

"Indeed, Mr. Fargo, why would I want to do a thing like that? I have only begun my quest to hunt the buffalo!"

"Your quest, as you call it, will be cut mighty short—along with your hair—if you don't hightail it." Fargo went on to explain what he had seen the night before, the huge number of Sioux warriors and their war dance.

"Fascinating," Compton said, his eyes sparkling with amusement. "Half-naked aboriginals dancing around a bonfire. I should have been there to see them. What a treat!"

"Not a treat. Any one of them would gladly lift your scalp for a trophy," Fargo said. He had feared Compton would brush off the warning as he did.

"Skye knows about these things, Mr. Compton," said Melissa. "We should heed his warning and—"

"And nothing," said Paul Hancock. "From what Fargo said, the Sioux are miles and miles to the west. We're heading north. They won't find us."

"I would rather like to see a native. That would be quite amusing," said Compton. Fargo watched the man carefully, trying to figure out his motives. Compton understood fully the threat they faced, yet he goaded both Melissa and Paul into continuing on a suicidal course.

"I don't know what riled them, but the Sioux are fixing to launch a big war. It might be against another tribe. They fight the Arapahos and Blackfeet all the time, but betting they aren't angry over what some white man's done and then crossing them is downright foolish."

"You have any guesses why they are on the warpath?" asked Paul.

"I don't know the Sioux language very well, but it sounded as if they've had enough of white prospectors moving into their hunting land to mine for gold. There was a lot of other talk I didn't follow."

"We are neither Arapaho nor gold miner," Compton said. "There is no reason for us to run off like silly geese. Find a spot to camp for the night. Then we can hunt for another herd of buffalo. Would you care to join in the sport, Mr. Fargo?"

"Gunning down buffalos you don't intend to eat isn't sporting," Fargo said.

"Then we shall all dine *very* well," Compton said, laughing. "I had Pierre fix the intestines as you suggested. They were a bit white and pasty, but utterly delicious. My compliments to you for suggesting such a fine dish."

"I'm glad you liked it," Fargo said coldly. "It might be your last meal if you don't leave now. You can put another ten miles between you and the Sioux camp before nightfall if you get rolling."

"I think not," Compton said, a steel edge coming into his voice. Lighter, he added, "I won't have my holiday ruined because of Indians."

"You might have more than that ruined," Fargo said.

Compton appeared not to hear him and barked orders for the driver to find a suitable spot for the evening encampment. As the wagon rattled along, Melissa hurriedly got to the rear, climbed over the gate, and jumped to the ground beside Fargo.

Fargo saw Compton's eyes narrow slightly, then the rich man went back to his map, Melissa and Fargo dismissed from all thought.

"You shouldn't anger him, Fargo," Paul said. "He'll fire Melissa and me."

"Count yourself lucky if he does," Fargo said. "I saw an entire village of Sioux and think there might be that many more around here. For all I know, you might be riding straight for their camp."

"What kind of scout are you, if you don't know?" asked Paul.

"Sorry to have bothered you," Fargo said. He turned to Melissa and said, "You should consider leaving these pigheaded fools to their fate and return to wherever you set out from."

"St. Louis," Melissa said.

"She's not going off alone with you," Paul said.

"Really, Paul," Melissa said to her brother. "I can take care of myself. It's apparent to just about everyone, Skye included, that we are not the rugged frontiersmen we led Mr. Compton to believe."

"He didn't know," Paul said defensively.

"I didn't know you'd never been farther west than St. Louis?" Fargo laughed. He settled down and said more somberly, "I've seen some fierce Indian uprisings. This has the makings of a big one, a violent one you don't want to be anywhere near. I don't care what Compton says, the Sioux aren't going to put on a show *for* you. Anything they do will be *to* you."

"Please, Paul, he listens to you because you're a man. Try to convince Mr. Compton of the danger."

Paul Hancock snorted and shuffled his feet in an unconscious imitation of a bull about to charge. Without another word, he stalked off to join Justin Compton in his wagon. Fargo wasn't sure what Paul was going to say, but it wasn't likely to be persuasive enough to get the man to turn his hunting expedition around and go back to civilization.

"What can we do, Skye?" asked Melissa. Her blue eyes fixed on his and held him as surely as if she had lassoed him.

"Keep out of sight and don't tempt fate. The Sioux are unforgiving."

"Wait," Melissa said, grabbing Fargo's arm. "Don't go. Don't leave us. Both of them, my brother and Mr. Compton, are pigheaded, like you said, but you can't leave us when we need your skills the most."

"I'm not a miracle worker. There's no way I can wave my arms and make the entire Sioux nation vanish. I'd sooner tackle a grizzly with nothing but my teeth."

"Stay the night, at least," Melissa insisted. "I'll talk to them both. Is there somewhere likely to be safer we might guide Mr. Compton?"

"He sounded pretty determined to hunt buffalo. Once you're off the basin and into the mountains, you don't find the big herds."

"What else is there to hunt?" Melissa was pleading with Fargo to provide her with alternatives that might entice Compton to safer ground.

"Elk, maybe," Fargo said. "The Laramie Mountains to the south are likely to have plenty of mule deer and even elk, but getting there would be more dangerous than staying put here." Fargo pictured the terrain in his mind and knew Compton and his party would probably come across Sioux scouts somewhere along the way. Continuing north toward the Dakota Territory was risky, too. The Sioux called that land their home.

The wagons ground to a halt and the servants began making camp. Fargo let Melissa hurry off to speak with her brother again, although that wasn't likely to change matters. When a man like Compton got his mind set, nothing changed it.

Especially know-nothings like Paul and Melissa Hancock.

Fargo mounted and rode in a wide circle around the camp, his sharp eyes peeled for any sign of Sioux raiding parties. The grasslands appeared as deserted as when he had ridden onto them days earlier, before seeing Paul Hancock.

For all the desolate expanse of gently waving grass mixed in with the burned areas, however, Fargo felt a tension in the air as if the entire region was going to explode and make the prairie fire and buffalo stampede look tame in comparison.

He returned to the campsite at dusk. The large fires sent curls of black smoke and dancing sparks high into the still evening sky that could be seen for miles. Fargo knew better than to argue with Compton over cold-camping, though. It would be a waste of breath.

"There you are, my good man," greeted Compton in his genial fashion. "Sit, have some of this fine ragout. Pierre has outdone himself. This is from the buffalo I shot." Compton put his nose close to a china plate brimming with the savory stew and inhaled deeply, then smacked his lips.

Fargo was so hungry that his belly rubbed against his spine. And truth be told, he did not look forward to another meal of beans and jerky chased down his gullet by tepid water from a canteen.

"Here, Mr. Fargo. Try some. Do, please," Melissa said, handing him a plate.

"This is mighty fancy china for the trail," Fargo said, running his finger around the gilt rim of the plate.

"I thought you would appreciate it. Some wine, Mr. Fargo?" asked Compton. He didn't wait for an answer but snapped his fingers to get a servant to bring a crystal glass filled to the brim with red wine. "Not the best combination, but who knows what wine best goes with buffalo meat, eh?" Compton grinned as Fargo sampled the tart wine, then put it down so he could attack the plate of buffalo stew.

"You can't expect me to give up more of this fine dining because of a native uprising, do you?"

"You know your own mind. I've told you how dangerous I think it is, and I've seen some massacres that would put you off your feed for a month of Sundays." Fargo shoveled in the food, wondering what he ought to do if Compton refused to find sanctuary.

"A proposition, Mr. Fargo. You don't seem to be heading toward any definite destination." When Fargo did not answer, Compton went on. "I can use a scout."

"What about them?" Fargo pointed his spoon toward Paul and Melissa.

"Mr. Hancock and his charming sister are marvelous companions. Call them repositories of information about this great land, if you will, but they are not *of* the land, if you catch my drift."

"They don't know diddly about scouting," Fargo said bluntly.

Compton laughed. "They have other endearing traits. If the menace posed by the natives—"

"The Sioux," Fargo corrected. It irritated him hearing the Indians called natives.

"Yes, of course, the Sioux," Compton said easily. "If they are such a threat, you can warn us in time to take cover or simply . . . run away."

"There might not be time for that. A determined Sioux warrior can ride sixty miles in a day. How far can you drive one of those fancy wagons?"

"Ten, if Bruno and Charles are adept at picking the right track to follow," Compton said. "But I do not intend racing the nat—the Sioux. Rather, I want them to slip past like a ghostly wind barely rippling the sheer lace curtains hanging in my window."

"But you'd like to see one of them?" prodded Fargo.

Compton smiled and nodded.

"So you want me to keep you away from the Sioux? What else?"

"Finding another buffalo herd would be exciting. However, I am more interested in the region to our north. The Belle Fourche, for instance, draws me strangely."

"A river?"

"I want to see a flowing river again, not some ridiculously small stream meandering across Thunder Basin."

Fargo wondered at Compton's knowledge of the region. It struck him as more precise than that owned up to by Paul Hancock.

"Are you looking for something in particular?" Fargo asked.

"I am a mere tourist out to take in the panorama of the West," Compton said insincerely. "Fifty dollars."

"What?"

"I'll pay fifty dollars a week to scout for my doughty expedition."

Fargo hardly believed his ears. That was more than the U.S. Army paid a scout for a month's service. He had been considering the offer of his scouting skills while he ate. This decided him.

"There've got to be some rules. If I tell you to run like hell, you don't stop to ask why. I'll have a reason but maybe not the time to explain."

"Agreed."

"Until I'm satisfied the Sioux are moving away, no

more fires that would give away the location of your camp."

"Oh, very well," Compton said, still amused.

"One more thing," Fargo said.

"What might this onerous request be?"

"You give your cook a raise. This is about the best plate of stew I've ever eaten."

"Done!" Justin Compton went off to keep his own company, leaving Fargo by the fire. Fargo kicked some dirt onto it causing it to sputter and die down a little. There was still too much smoke, but he knew there wasn't anything he could do about that. Buffalo chips were the best fuel to be found on the generally treeless grassland, and they always smoked and sent sparks aloft, depending on what the buffalo had been eating and how the chip had dried.

"I'll take that," came a soft voice.

"Thanks," Fargo said, handing Melissa his plate. She put it down on a rock beside the fire and looked at him.

"Mr. Compton said he had hired you to scout for us."

"I don't want that to cause trouble with your brother."

Melissa looked startled for a moment, then chuckled.

"Paul has mixed feelings about you. Saving his life twice makes him beholden to you, but he thinks you have other reasons for hanging around."

"What might those be?" Fargo asked. He liked the way the conversation was going. Compton offered top dollar to work for him, but the possibility of female company was a bonus Fargo had hoped for but had not really expected.

"I want to see some of this wide-open country. Come with me?"

"I'd be pleased to show it to you, ma'am." Fargo held out his arm and Melissa locked hers through it. Together they walked away from camp. Fargo was alert for the sound of anything unusual moving across the grasslands, but he became increasingly distracted as Melissa moved closer and her hip rubbed seductively against his.

"It's astounding how you can walk a few yards and be so alone," Melissa said, letting Fargo put his arm around her and pull her even closer. Fargo felt the crush of her tender breast against his chest. Then all he noticed was the way his pulse raced.

"We could be alone, with it seeming like there was nary a soul alive in the rest of Wyoming," he said. He turned the woman in the circle of his arms and looked down into her twinkling blue eyes for a moment. Then he kissed her.

At first there was a touch of awkwardness. They pressed and moved, broke off slightly as if Melissa was unsure of herself, then she returned his kiss with more passion and fervor than he would have thought was locked up inside her.

His hands roved up and down her back, touching here and there and feeling her begin to respond totally to him. When they broke off the kiss again, they were both breathless.

"Yes, Skye," she said in a husky whisper. "Yes!"

Fargo had not come prepared for this eventuality, although he knew he should have. If they wanted a blanket they would have to return to camp. He knew that would never do, especially if Melissa's brother was on the lookout for them. He still mistrusted Fargo with his sister.

With good reason.

Fargo unbuckled his gun belt and dropped it. Then he unfastened his trousers and let out the raging beast that had started to make him so uncomfortable.

"Oh my," was all Melissa said when she saw what popped from his trousers. She took it in her hand and began stroking up and down. "So long, so thick," she murmured. "Do you want me to kiss it?"

"Go on," Fargo said. He swallowed hard when he felt the woman's lips lightly caress the tip of his manhood. Then Melissa's ruby lips opened slightly as she took in the entire end of his shaft. Her tongue restlessly prowled the knoblike head, then began moving down the sensitive underside until Fargo found himself shifting weight from one foot to the other and back as his body caught fire.

He stroked her long, lustrous dark hair as her head bobbed over his groin. The tiny prickling sensation in his loins grew until he was hotter than a prairie fire. Fargo liked what Melissa did for him, but there had to be more. He laced his fingers through the raven locks and tilted her head up slightly.

"You don't like what I'm doing?" she asked. Her hot breath thrilled Fargo as it gusted all around him.

"I love it, but I want to give you something in return."

"Like this?" She seized his shaft and squeezed hard. He took a deep breath to control himself. Everything she did to him sent new bolts of lightning coursing through his body.

"Yes," he said, gently lifting her up. "I think this might work so we both can enjoy it." He sank to his knees. Melissa bit her lower lip as he slid his hands under her skirts and began working up the slender, warm pillars of her legs. He ran his hands between her thighs and gently parted them so her stance was wider than usual.

"Go on, Skye. Go on!" she urged.

He hiked the skirts up around the beautiful woman's waist and exposed her nether regions to the fitfully blowing, warm night breezes. But he gave her no time to complain. Reaching around, he cupped her buttocks and then gripped down hard as he lifted.

"Ohhh!" Melissa cried as Fargo stood and swept her off her feet. Her legs went wide and circled his body. Fargo had to lift her a little higher and then let her settle down in the most delightful way possible.

For a moment, neither said anything. They simply enjoyed being locked together so intimately. Then Fargo felt himself pulse and jerk in the warmth of Melissa's tight, moist channel. He was going to have difficulty controlling himself because her every movement stimulated him more and more.

"This is paradise, Skye," she cooed. Then she wiggled her hips and squeezed down with strong inner muscles. Fargo felt like he was being milked.

He swung the woman around, her hair flying out in a dark swath to hide the night-cloaked Wyoming grasslands. Around and around they whirled, Fargo holding her firmly to his groin. Melissa tightened her legs around his waist and snuggled down an extra inch onto his fleshy spike. The faster they turned, the more aroused Fargo became.

From the way Melissa moaned and sobbed, she liked riding the carousel just as much.

Fargo slowed the spinning and bent forward. Somehow, Melissa's blouse had come unbuttoned, exposing the luscious mounds of her tender breasts. Fargo licked and sucked and nipped at the hardened caps atop each breast. When his lips tightened on one and he drew it fully into his mouth so he could run his tough tongue over it, he felt a quaking begin in Melissa's body that could not be stopped.

She rammed her hips down hard and began rotating in small, insistent circles. When the dark-haired woman threw her head back and let out a howl to rival any mating coyote's, Fargo knew he was giving as good as he was getting.

The trembling abated in her body, and Melissa melted a little. Fargo gripped her rump tighter and began lifting and pulling with smooth, easy motions. Every time she slid away, a bit of his manhood was exposed. Then he drew her back; each tug delivered with growing power and insistence until he vanished entirely up into her most intimate passage.

The force was not as great as if they had been lying on a blanket. But what it lacked in sheer power it made up for in the different ways he entered and left her. Once completely inside her, Fargo began moving her hips around in such a way that he felt like a spoon in a mixing bowl.

The pressure and liquid warmth began to take its toll on him. He held back until he felt the earthquake starting once more in the woman's responsive loins. She clamped down around him so tightly he thought he had been trapped in a mine-shaft collapse.

Sweat beading both their faces, they moved together the best they could, deriving friction from their coupling until neither could hold back an instant longer. The shudders that had begun in Melissa's body spread down Fargo's length and set off the volcanic tide in his loins.

He clung fiercely to her and thrust and turned and moved and did everything he could to join them together in body and soul.

Fargo grunted as he spilled his seed into her yearning cavity. Melissa flushed from her breasts to her shoulders and face. Then she sobbed, sighed, and fell limp in his strong arms.

He slowly lowered her until she could get her feet under her. Even then he continued to hold her, kissing her face and lips and hair and breasts.

"Oh, Skye," Melissa said in a low voice. "I never thought it would be *that* good."

"It was better than that," he told her.

She rested her cheek against him. They said nothing more. Their bodies had already said everything worth saying.

6

"No, no, Fargo," Paul Hancock said anxiously. "Mr. Compton doesn't want to go that way. He said we were to scout ahead in that direction, toward the hills."

"This will be easier travel for the wagons," Fargo insisted. All day long Hancock had been crossing him and trying to make him change the route he was scouting. "Do you have any idea what it's like for a wagon to break an axle out here? It could take the better part of a day to fix, if you have a spare. Longer if we have to find a tree to cut a new axle. Which would Compton prefer? Being stranded for a day or getting to the river?"

"He does want to get to the Belle Fourche as fast as possible."

"Then we go this way. It might look longer to travel, but we'll get to the river faster."

"I don't know," Hancock said reluctantly.

"How much scouting and guide work have you really done?" Fargo asked, finally reaching the point where bluntness served him better than waiting for Paul and his sister to drop little tidbits of information in front of him like bread crumbs in front of a pigeon. He had a pretty good idea what the answer was going to be, but he wanted Hancock to come clean and admit his inexperience.

"Not much," Paul said. "Hell, Fargo, you know the answer already. None at all. Melissa and I came across Mr. Compton in St. Louis and saw a meal ticket."

"You lied to him?"

"He lied to us," Paul said defensively. Fargo wanted to add that Compton probably liked having Melissa around more than her brother, but he kept quiet. If he said anything now Paul might clam up.

They rode in silence for another ten minutes, Paul stewing in his own juices and Fargo carefully noting the lay of the land and memorizing it so he could draw a map later for either of Compton's drivers, Bruno or Charles, to follow.

"Does it show?" Paul asked unexpectedly.

"That you don't know what you're doing? Only to someone who's been on the range for a day or two."

"I was afraid you'd say that. I reckon we'd never have fooled anyone more experienced, would we?" Paul laughed ruefully. "The truth was, Melissa and I were starving to death. Our parents died of cholera and there wasn't a whole lot left afterward."

Fargo wondered if Paul and Melissa had squandered their inheritance or if their legacy had not been too large to start with.

"We tried to do a dozen different jobs, but there wasn't much call for two educated people who, well, who had never worked before."

"Schoolmarm," Fargo said. "The number of people who can read out West is pretty small. Every settlement that gets built puts up a church, a town hall, and then a schoolhouse. There's quite a demand for book learning and whoever can teach it."

"Melissa's not up to it. Neither am I, for that matter. We were considering doing something truly dreadful when Mr. Compton came along."

"Turning to thievery?" asked Fargo. He saw the flush rising on Paul's face and knew the answer. Fargo doubted the Hancocks would have been any better bilking the gullible than they were at scouting.

"We were desperate," Paul said. "Somehow, we said the right things to Mr. Compton and he asked us to lead his expedition."

"How did you know enough to convince him you had all that experience on the frontier?" asked Fargo, interested now. He had not figured out what made Justin Compton tick yet, but the man was no fool. He was a rich man's son, a scion of great wealth, but he was not the sort to be easily duped by the likes of Paul and Melissa Hancock.

"Melissa, mostly. She reads a great deal. Frémont diaries were of particular help in convincing Mr. Compton we were far more competent than we are. I also mentioned that Jesse Benton Frémont was an acquaintance."

"You and your family hobnobbed with the daughter of a U.S. senator? Maybe that is why Compton asked you along on this little pageant of his, for the political connections."

"We haven't seen Mrs. Frémont since she married. I doubt she would even remember us. But she is a vivid writer of redoubtable skill, and I admire the exploits of her husband greatly."

Fargo digested this information as they rode up to the top of a hill. By his reckoning the river lay a dozen miles to the northwest, a direction he wanted to avoid if possible. The Sioux war party he had spied on had been due west, but a gut feeling told him the real damage lay farther north. If they went directly to the Belle Fourche River, he suspected they would find the rest of the Sioux on the warpath.

"The river runs from the northwest downward across the Wyoming plains to the southwest," Fargo said. "We can head north or even a bit to the northeast and come on it in a couple days."

"Mr. Compton was impatient to get there," Paul said.

"Ten miles a day with those wagons is a good clip," Fargo said. "The grasslands appear flat but the ravines cut by spring runoff and summer rains slow down travel. Wind looks agreeable blowing through the tall grass, but it also cuts washboard furrows in the ground."

"Fargo, I, uh, would you mind if I told Mr. Compton I had found the route?"

"So you can earn your money?"

"Something like that," Paul said. "It's Melissa, too. She knows I'm no good at this. She helps Pierre with the cooking and mends and does all sorts of useful things. Me, I've been pretty worthless up till now."

Fargo didn't bother with his opinion that Hancock was still pretty worthless. Compton had not made the fifty-dollar weekly salary contingent on him performing any definite duties so he saw no reason not to let Paul take credit for the day's work.

He still worried more about the Sioux than their travel route.

"Go on," Fargo said. "If you return to camp, do you think you can show the way this far while I scout ahead?"

"Of course, yes, thanks, Fargo. I really appreciate it." Humming to himself, Paul turned his horse and trotted back along the trail they had left. Fargo had not bothered trying to cover their tracks, and even Paul ought to be observant enough to find his way back.

Fargo watched as the man disappeared down the hill and into the grasslands. For a basin that appeared flat as a table, there were a surprising number of places to simply vanish. He turned his attention back to the land between him and the river.

In the distance to the east Fargo spotted a dust cloud billowing. From the way it swirled he knew no wind had raised it. Hooves, many hooves, kicked up the land and created the small storm. He wished he had a spyglass to see better, then decided it did not matter. Those were not Indians to the east. If he had to make a guess, buffalos would be top of the list.

Compton might be interested in bagging another buffalo. And if he wasn't, Fargo might convince him to go hunting since the herd was far to the east, away from where he suspected the Sioux to be gathering for their war.

Fargo snapped the reins and got the stallion moving down the far side of the gradual hill and quickly found himself in rugged terrain. Zigzagging back and forth brought him a mile or so farther, where he stopped to listen intently.

Although he heard nothing, Fargo's keen sense of smell picked up a hint of smoke. Unlike the choking black smoke produced by the prairie fire as it ravaged the grasslands, this smoke was earthier.

"Buffalo dung," he decided. "Sioux."

He turned slowly and homed in on the smoke drifting toward him from the direction of the river. It made sense that the Sioux would camp near the Belle Fourche since it provided fresh water and fish for a large number of braves, their squaws, and children.

Riding slowly, keeping as low a profile as he could amid the waist-high grass, Fargo began hearing faint sounds from a village. He dismounted and secured his Ovaro to a clump of yucca; then he advanced on foot to see how much trouble Compton would be in if he barged on through to the river.

Fargo caught his breath when four braves rode past. He sank down low in the grass and waited to see if he had been found out. The four were riding at a quick gait, anxious to reach their tepees. Fargo found their trail through the grass and advanced on a parallel course until he spotted the tops of a half-dozen tepees. Curls of smoke twisted skyward, and the sounds of a large group told him he had not stumbled across a small hunting party. This was a village equal in size to the other he had seen.

Fargo crawled on his belly through the grass until he reached a spot where he could peer out. He started counting horses and gave up after he reached fifty. There had to be at least that many tepees, although the squaws and children were nowhere to be seen. Warriors decked out in paint strutted around, pounding their chests and boasting.

This was enough for Fargo. He slipped away, found his horse, and rode as fast as he could for Compton's camp. It was suicide to go directly for the river, and angling to the northeast as he had intended might not be such a good idea either. The river was blocked until the Sioux moved on.

He arrived at the camp only a few minutes after Hancock. Fargo wondered if Paul had gotten lost on the way back but did not ask. He was too intent on guiding Compton away from the Sioux village.

"So you think there is a chance we can reach the river

in a day or so?" Compton asked Hancock. Before Paul could answer, Fargo cut in.

"I saw another band of Sioux warriors. A big one cutting us off from the Belle Fourche."

"I do want to see them," Compton said, rubbing his hands together. "Perhaps we could shoot it out with them."

"That might provide good parlor talk back in New York," Fargo said, "but to brag on it, you have to live to tell about it. There're hundreds of armed warriors. Shoot at one and you get the rest after you, ready to lift your scalp."

"Deliciously put, sir," Compton said.

"How would you like to get another buffalo for your stewpot?" Fargo asked, changing the subject immediately when he saw Compton was at least half serious about continuing to the river so he could run afoul of the Sioux.

"An excellent idea! Why, Pierre has been making threats about boiling the weeds all around and forcing me to eat it unless he gets fresh meat. When can we go?"

Fargo sucked in a deep breath, then let it out. The die was cast. He had deflected Compton's collision course with the Indians. It was up to him to see that Compton stayed far from the Sioux camp and continued to enjoy his curious odyssey across the Wyoming grasslands.

"We can set out right away," Compton said.

"It's getting late," Fargo pointed out.

"Let the rest remain with the wagons. You and I, Mr. Fargo, will be at the herd at first light for a delightful hunt!"

Fargo looked at Paul and shook his head in amazement. Justin Compton continued to confound him.

"Are you coming with us?" Fargo asked Paul.

"I—he didn't say anything about me going," Paul said, obviously tossed on the horns of a dilemma. "As much as I feel obligated to ride with you, I should stay in camp with Melissa. Will the Sioux come this way?"

"They were camped near the river. Unless something spooked them, I don't think they will stray far from their source of water and food." Even as Fargo spoke, he started worrying about the Sioux hunters spotting the same buffalo herd he had and riding to supply meat for their families. If they went after the buffalos, the Indians and Compton would cross paths.

"Tallyho, Mr. Fargo," called Compton. He was already mounted and lifted his heavy rifle to show his eagerness to be chasing after the buffalos. "Time's a-wasting!"

Fargo saw Melissa near the supply wagon. She smiled at him and waved good-bye almost shyly, then hurried off before anyone in Compton's party spotted her. It did not pay for them to be too open about what had happened out on the prairie. A woman's reputation got stained fast and irrevocably if it got out she did things like Melissa and Fargo had done.

Fargo wondered what Compton would think if he found out.

"Which way, Mr. Fargo? Which way do we go to shoot a mountain of succulent buffalo flesh?"

"That way," Fargo said, pointing almost due east. They could ride out onto the grasslands, then cut north and be sure to avoid the Sioux.

After thirty minutes, it grew darker, but Compton took no notice, riding on as if he had an owl's night vision. Finally Fargo had to call an end to their trip.

"I don't want my horse stepping into a prairie-dog hole in the dark."

"But we should get closer. I can almost smell the woolly brutes." Compton stuck his nose into the air and sniffed, as if he could locate the herd that way. With the wind blowing from their back, it was more likely the buffalos would smell their hunters than the other way around.

Before Fargo could say a word, he heard the unmistakable bellowing sound of a bull.

"Get your rifle ready," Fargo said. "That one's close."

"It's a big one, isn't it?" asked Compton. "I can tell by the sound."

"It's big," Fargo said. He hoped the bull wasn't fighting off a younger male for dominance in the herd. Getting caught in such a fight meant added danger.

Compton swung his rifle around, drew out a tripod from a holder beneath the barrel, and pulled back the heavy hammer. He nodded once to Fargo, showing he was ready for the kill. Fargo hesitated when he saw the determination in the man's face. Seconds before, Compton had been flighty, almost giddy about the prospect of shooting another buffalo. There was nothing in his demeanor now but the calm, focused assurance of an experienced hunter.

"Not too far ahead," Fargo said, peering into the gathering gloom. "It'll be a hard shot in the dark."

"No need to worry about that," Compton said, driving his tripod legs into the ground and balancing his rifle in the fork atop. "My vision is perfect, as is my aim."

Fargo started to caution Compton against excessive confidence, when the man's rifle barked and a two-foot-long orange flame burst from the muzzle. The report set Fargo's ears to ringing, and he blinked a few times to clear his sight of the dancing orange and blue dots from the muzzle flash.

"That was a fine shot," Compton congratulated himself. He lifted the heavy rifle from the fork, folded the tripod, and inserted it into the holder beneath the barrel.

Fargo stared into the gloom in wonder. The bull was nowhere to be seen. He made certain Compton had his rifle stored before going on foot in the direction he had seen the buffalo. More than a hundred yards off, he almost fell over the carcass.

He examined the bison and saw that Compton's bullet had caught the beast in the shoulder. It had been a clean, instant-kill shot. Fargo could not have done better himself—and under the conditions, he might not have been as lucky in his shot placement.

Or was it luck? He studied Justin Compton as the man came up to claim his trophy. There was much about the man Fargo wanted to know and had yet to learn.

7

"I want another," Compton said, putting his boot on the buffalo's haunch and leaning forward slightly, as if he expected a photographer to capture the moment.

"You must have a big trophy room," Fargo said. He considered what to do with the downed buffalo. They couldn't haul it back to the wagons. If he started dressing it out now that twilight was turning to impenetrable night, he risked attracting wolves and coyotes with the blood odor.

"A huge one," Compton solemnly assured him. "You should see some of the heads I've taken. No human ones, though," Compton said with a laugh. From the sound of it, Fargo wasn't sure if Compton regretted that omission. "Why don't you come back East with me when I am done with this primitive terrain? You would be an immediate allurement to the rather bored stratum of society I travel in." Compton saw that Fargo wasn't paying him any attention and hefted his rifle, tilting his head to listen himself. "What is it, Mr. Fargo?"

"Hoofbeats," Fargo said. "A ways off. That direction." He turned so the wind blew gently against his face. The faint sounds had caught on the breeze and drifted to his sensitive ears. He caught the noise again and made out at least three riders.

"Indians? I would enjoy meeting a redskin savage."

"No, you wouldn't," Fargo said curtly, "but I don't think those are Sioux. If they were hunting the same herd this bull came from, they would be farther toward the river. Instead, they are out on the plains coming this way."

"Perhaps they are ranging to the east for some other reason and are now returning to their encampment."

"They wouldn't cross the basin unless there was a good reason. No water for their horses," Fargo said.

"How many can there be?" demanded Compton. "I barely hear them. If the entire Sioux nation was mounted and on the move, the very earth ought to shake!"

Fargo didn't bother sharing his supposition of only a handful of riders. Compton was right about one thing. If all the Sioux were moving, there would be more than a few faint hoofbeats. He came to a quick decision on what to do.

"I'll go scout and see if I can spot them before they find us. Stay with the buffalo. Will your wagon drivers come at daybreak?"

"Bruno and Charles are good men," Compton said with his superior air. "I have no idea what Mr. Hancock might advise them to do or how they might respond." Compton smiled a little when he added, "I am sure both Charles and Bruno would do whatever Miss Hancock asked of them, though. She has the manner about her."

"You might want to abandon the kill and go straight back to your camp," Fargo said. "Either way, you'll be all right."

"I could come with you to see who these mysterious marauders are," Compton said. "That would give me a great thrill, skulking about as we stalk the stalkers!"

"Either stay here or go back to your camp," Fargo said firmly. "You'd only put us both at risk." Fargo swung into the saddle. His Ovaro tossed its head and seemed reluctant to go find who the riders might be. The paint's instincts had aided Fargo more than once. Considering the horse's reluctance, he changed his mind about what was best for Justin Compton.

"I'll go back to camp and fetch the wagons," Fargo said. "Stay with your kill, don't wander around, and be very sure of what's out there before taking a potshot at it." He pointed into the night.

"Should I build a fire?"

Fargo was torn on that. A fire kept coyotes and packs

of wolves at bay if they scented the buffalo, but it also attracted unwanted attention from two-legged varmints.

"Too risky. Keep a sharp lookout for wolves. If they want the buffalo, let them have it."

"I say, that's not fair. I shot this woolly behemoth for—"

"You don't have enough ammo to keep a hungry wolf pack at bay. No one does." Fargo's words penetrated. He had not come out and declared that Compton would end up part of the lupine meal, but the man was smart enough to figure it out. He nodded agreement.

Fargo turned and guided his Ovaro through the darkness as fast as he could ride in the direction of Compton's camp. He felt as if some unseen disaster was rushing up on him that he was powerless to stop.

To his surprise and dismay, the wagon drivers had not camped for the night but had slowly followed Fargo's and Compton's trail through the dark. Bruno walked ahead of the lead wagon, a torch held high to light the tracks. Fargo saw Paul driving the first wagon, with Melissa beside him. Charles and the sullen chef, Pierre, rode in the box of the second wagon.

"Why didn't you camp?" Fargo asked Paul Hancock in exasperation. "It's dangerous traveling at night."

"I remember what you said about breaking an axle, Fargo," Paul said, "but Bruno insisted that we go after Mr. Compton."

"Why didn't you talk some sense into them?" Fargo asked Melissa. From her expression he saw that she was the reason they had started on this dangerous night-time trip.

"Don't be angry, Skye," she said as he stopped alongside the wagon. "I got spooked. There's somebody out there, and I thought it was safer to keep moving."

"Paul," Fargo said. "Did you tell her what I said about breaking an axle?"

"Yes, he did," Melissa said quickly, cutting off her brother. "I know there aren't any trees out here suitable to repair damage, but this seemed . . . more important."

"Compton's a couple of miles away," Fargo said, not

wanting to argue the point. What was done was done. "Bruno's got a good eye for tracking in the dark." He scowled at the man's torch sending a constant cloud of darting, dancing fireflylike sparks into the night. The grasslands were dry and another prairie fire could doom them all.

"Stay with us," Skye," urged Melissa. "The others claim it's my imagination, but I've heard riders. I never spotted them, but I know they are there. I feel it in my bones."

"Pierre doesn't like her," Paul said. "He thinks she meddles too much."

"Too many cooks spoil the broth," Fargo said. He chewed on his lower lip a moment as he decided what to do. There was little danger to the people in the wagons that they didn't bring on themselves. He worried more about leaving Justin Compton alone with the buffalo. Too many dangers stalked Thunder Basin at night for Fargo not to fret over leaving a tenderfoot to his own devices.

"I'll meet you where Compton shot his buffalo. It'll be easy finding the camp if you keep going in this direction. Look for a fire."

"Skye!" called Melissa, reaching out to him. Then she settled back and folded her hands in her lap. "Be careful," she said.

He respectfully touched the brim of his hat, nodded politely in her direction, and lit out for the spot where he had left Compton. Fargo was not certain what he would find when he got to the large buffalo carcass, but his fears were groundless. Rising from behind the bulk of meat came Justin Compton.

"You weren't gone long, Mr. Fargo. I trust you are not returning with bad news." Compton tucked a notebook into his shirt and buttoned it up. Fargo wondered what the man had been writing. Details of his kill, possibly. He ignored such speculation as he dismounted and looked around.

"Gather buffalo chips. We need a fire so Bruno can find us more easily. He and Charles started out on their own."

"With Miss Hancock's blessing, I suspect," Compton said, laughing heartily. "It is good to know she worries so, and that she can't bear to be away from me for any length of time."

Fargo didn't bother to contradict him. He said nothing as he dug a fire pit and began tossing in the dried buffalo dung Compton had gathered. A few handfuls of dried grass and he was ready to start the fire using his flint and steel. As Compton watched with real interest, Fargo nursed a fitful spark into a decent fire.

"Can we cook some of this meat?" asked Compton.

"Go ahead," Fargo said, adding more buffalo chips to the fire so that its flames rose to almost waist level. The amount of choking smoke from the fire forced Fargo back a few paces.

"Would you care to start butchering?" asked Compton.

"I want to look for the wagons," Fargo said. He also wanted to see if he could spot the riders he had heard earlier, which had also spooked Melissa Hancock. Fargo was sure she was not jumping at shadows any more than he was.

Fargo went a few yards into the dark, then began circling. He froze and stared across the starlit grassland at a silhouetted rider. For a moment Fargo thought his eyes were playing tricks on him, that he looked at a low-growing scrub oak that only appeared to be a mounted man. Then the horse turned, and the rider snapped the reins and vanished.

Fargo doubted the distant pilgrim could have missed the blazing fire. Men got strange notions on the frontier. Most were accustomed to being alone for long weeks, but what man turned away from a short conversation or a shared meal when he could leave at any time? Even the worst hermit Fargo had found during years of roaming the mountains ventured forth to stare at his fellow man, if only to indulge in a few minutes of shouted invective.

Reaching the area where he had seen the rider, Fargo looked around but saw nothing to show he had not been duped by a mirage. But no mirage came out on a moonless night. Fargo would sooner believe he had seen a ghost than think he was seeing things.

The clank and clatter of wagons distracted him. He wheeled the Ovaro around and walked back to where Compton greeted his servants jovially. Compton pointed to the carcass and ordered Pierre to get to work on it immediately. To Fargo's surprise, Compton had begun butchering the carcass and had not done a bad job. A small steak broiled over the fire and made his nose twitch with the fragrance of fresh meat cooking.

He looked at the man with some respect and wondered about Compton's need to hire frauds like Paul and Melissa Hancock to guide him through the West.

"It's like a mountain," Melissa said in awe, staring at the mound of dead buffalo. "What must it have been like when it was alive?"

"A ravaging beast with hooves the size of dinner plates," Compton said pretentiously. "As it ran, its monstrous bulk shook the very roots of the planet. But it was no match for me." He acted out how he had leveled his rifle and brought down the bull.

Fargo let Compton continue his recitation of the kill to Melissa and went to talk with her brother. Paul worked to get their gear out of the back of the wagon he had been driving.

"Did you see any outriders?" Fargo asked.

"Of course not," Paul said. "That was what Melissa imagined, not me." He tried to sound unconcerned. He failed. "Y-you don't believe her, do you, Fargo? That someone's out there?"

"Learn to respect your sister's intuition," Fargo said. He checked his Colt, then mounted. "I'll be back before sunrise. Don't take a potshot at me when I return—but be sure it's me."

"There *was* someone out there," Paul said, shivering. "I'll keep a sharp watch, Fargo. I promise."

Fargo rode from camp, Compton still regaling Melissa with the details of his kill. As he rode over a low ridge, he saw the man giving her a bit of the buffalo meat he had just cooked. She took it daintily but ate avidly, her attention on the hunter and his tales of courage.

Out of sight of the camp, away from the cheery campfire and mouthwatering cooking odors, Fargo found himself in a different world. The night closed in with finality around him and the wind that had blown softly across Thunder Basin now whipped at his face and hands, carrying just a hint of cold with it.

He considered riding back to the spot where he had seen the other rider, then discarded the notion. Finding the precise spot in the dark was a fool's errand. Fargo had another idea. Someone was out here—he was sure of it—and it was easier to let them come to him than for him to find them.

Fargo rode along the back trail, ranging from one side to the other, as he kept his eyes peeled for any trace of the mysterious riders.

He drew rein and sat motionless when he saw two men a hundred feet off kneeling down to examine the cut-up ground where the wagons had rolled less than an hour earlier. One man looked up, then shot to his feet. Fargo didn't catch what he said, but the other man jumped onto his horse. The two of them galloped off.

Honest men weren't that skittish. These two acted like boys caught with their hands in a cookie jar. They were following Compton for a reason—and Fargo intended to find out what it was. He might get answers from them that he hadn't gotten from the Hancocks or Compton himself.

Rather than gallop after the men, Fargo cut to the east and followed a dry riverbed. It provided safer footing for his horse and kept him from getting tangled in the low-growing vegetation along the wagon route. The riverbed angled back in the direction of the riders. Fargo did not push his Ovaro but let it have its head, making better progress than the men he chased.

He found himself crossing the tracks left by the wagon before the riders reached that point. Fargo unshipped his Henry rifle and waited for the pair of horsemen to come into sight. Less than a minute after he levered a round into the Henry, he saw the men coming over a rise.

"Hold it there, gents," Fargo called out. "I've got a few questions for you."

Fargo lifted the rifle to his shoulder to emphasize how much he wanted answers from them when he got a chill that ran up and down his spine. He ducked forward fast. The bullet singing its way through the night barely missed hitting him in the back of the head.

Fargo saw that he was caught between two groups of riders. The men he had tried to stop were unlimbering their six-shooters and the two behind him already had their weapons out and firing.

He needed to get to cover fast or he'd end up as dead as the bull buffalo Compton had brought down.

8

Foot-long tongues of orange flame licked toward Fargo. He ducked low and put his heels to the Ovaro's flanks as bullets flew by him. There was no way he could out-fight two separate groups of gunmen, one company on each side catching him in a cross fire. They probably rode together, and he had had a touch of bad luck getting between them before they rejoined, but that didn't make it any less deadly for him.

"After him!" came the distant cry from farther along the trail. "We can't let him get away!"

Fargo knew the men were serious and thought it was time to show them he had teeth—and could use them.

He turned in the saddle and looked behind. The dark masked the actual number of men after him, but he thought it was as many as five. He had made the right decision before by not shooting it out with them. Now he hoped luck would smile in his direction as he took a few over-the-shoulder shots. Fargo swung his Henry around, aimed the best he could from the back of a galloping horse and squeezed the trigger. The recoil nudged his shoulder, and the bullet whined past the closest rider.

Fargo let out a whoop of triumph when he saw the man jerk around, arms akimbo as he tried to reach for his six-shooter and grab air at the same time. Whether he had hit the man or simply had come close enough to make him react didn't matter. Fargo had taken him out of the saddle and left him struggling in the dust.

"Les, you look after Stack," came the loud command from a rider in the back of the pack chasing him. Fargo had knocked out one and removed a second from the chase, but he had not stopped their leader.

Fargo got off another shot, but it went wide. Then came a whistling hail of lead that forced him to stop his wild shooting so he could tend to riding. One slug grazed the Ovaro's hindquarters and caused it to buck and try to rear. Fargo kept the horse running at breakneck speed through the darkness as he sought a way to shake off the three men still hot on his heels.

The stallion, powerful as it was, began to tire. With three men behind him, Fargo knew time was short for him to do anything. He veered to the south, trying to throw them off his trail. Reining in, he gave his horse a rest while he listened intently for sounds of pursuit. Fargo breathed a little easier, thinking he had gotten away until he heard the soft clop-clop-clop of hooves as the gunmen methodically hunted for the spot where he had turned from his beeline-straight course away from the ambush.

He dismounted and waited for the men to find his trail. On foot, with his Henry, he was more than a match for them. Fargo wondered about the man he had shot. If the wound was serious, that meant the man's partner would stay to tend him. That took two of them away from future gunfights. If he had only unseated the man, he might face all five again.

The uncertainty was nothing new for Fargo, but he began to get antsy when he realized they were only a few miles from Compton's camp. If Compton—or Paul Hancock—heard the shots, he might come to investigate. Fargo was having a hard enough time outmaneuvering the gunmen with only his own scalp at stake. Having to look after a greenhorn who had no idea what it was like to face another man with a gun would tip the scales out of his favor.

Fargo waited almost ten minutes, watching his back trail for the riders to appear. When they didn't, he mounted again and looked at the stars to get his bearings. The only thing worse than Compton or Hancock blundering in on this turkey shoot was Fargo leading the gunmen back to the camp.

He hadn't figured out who the five were, but they were inclined to shoot first and never ask questions. Fargo thought they might be outlaws intent on robbing anyone they came across on the prairie. If so, they would find easy pickings at Compton's camp. Fargo had to be sure they never circled close enough to get the scent of such wealth.

He went east, in the direction the riders had come from, thinking to get behind them and then cut north to escape them. For almost twenty minutes he thought he had eluded the outlaws. Then Fargo got a prickly feeling that caused the hairs on the back of his neck to rise. Something was not right.

Stopping, he stood in the stirrups to give himself a better view of the dark grasslands. The wind that had promised to chill his flesh earlier had died, leaving the basin in an unnatural stillness broken only by distant coyote howls. His keen eyes took in every detail of the land and finally fixed on a gently sloping hillside several yards away. Fargo could not tell what caused him to stare so intently at the dark lumps there—until one moved.

The riders had paced his retreat, either with incredible skill or through sheer luck, finding him again.

One shadow moved and was soon joined by a second and finally a third. Fargo touched the Henry rifle and considered the distance. The shot during the day would be difficult. At night it was nothing but blind luck if he hit any of them. Worse than missing, he would alert them to his position. Fargo was not certain they had spotted him. They might just be riding along searching for him.

Then he realized they had found him as surely as he had located them. The three turned as one and rode slowly in his direction, as if they could sneak up and take him unaware.

The Trailsman knew every trick for concealing his tracks, but most took time to implement. It would only be moments before the trio got close enough to throw lead at him with accuracy.

If he made his stand, he might pick off one or even two of them. Fargo could not hope that would drive away the third. With slugs flying blindly in the night, he ran the big risk of catching lead himself. Fargo made his decision. He turned his paint and headed northeast, walking the Ovaro and trying to hold noise down to a minimum. When he topped a rise, he urged the horse to a trot and changed direction, heading directly north and using the land as a shield to hide his retreat. As he rode, Fargo counted off the seconds until he got to three hundred, then drew rein and halted so he could listen. The sounds of his horse had been muffled by the grassy rise, but not after the outlaws crested the top and came down on this side.

Fargo knew the sound of his horse's hooves would echo along the lay of the land and let them know exactly where he had ridden.

It worked the other way, too. He heard the telltale clatter the instant the three riders started down the gentle slope after him. Fargo doubted they had supernatural powers. They had to follow him as much on instinct as through skill. The stars cast too wan a light for easy hunting, even by the most eagle-eyed tracker. With the occasional high, feathery cloud drifting across the sky, dimming even this pale white illumination, the only sure way of tracking was to wait for dawn to find the grass crushed by hooves.

Fargo hoped the three gunmen would do just that. If so, he would be long gone and back at Compton's camp in an hour to alert them of the danger.

As he sat and waited to see what the outlaws would do, Fargo thought hard on his situation. What was the danger? Would the riders attack a camp if the warning had been given? Were these even outlaws? There was a faint chance this might be a posse hunting for an outlaw. The distance had been too great for Fargo to see any badges pinned to their vests, but that didn't mean they weren't there.

But he didn't think they were lawmen. Even if they were after real desperadoes, he doubted a marshal would order his men to open fire the instant he spotted an unidentified rider on the plains. Fargo had nothing to lose assuming the worst—that these men were bandits.

He canted his head to the side and caught every sound coming his way. He bit off a curse of frustration when it became obvious that they weren't quitting for the night. Fargo thought they had split up, one going in the other direction and two coming toward him as they sought his tracks.

"Hey, Jesse! Come on back!"

"What'd ya find? His trail?" came a fainter reply.

"Yep."

Fargo thought the pair immediately behind him would ride slower, waiting for their partner to rejoin them. That gave him a few minutes to find a good spot for an ambush and shoot them out of the saddle. Two against one would prove lopsided odds—for Fargo. But doubt still gnawed at him that these men might have a legitimate reason for chasing after him the way they were. If they weren't lawmen, and he had no way of knowing without surrendering to them, they might be cowboys from a nearby ranch hunting down rustlers. A dozen other possibilities raced through his mind.

They might be honest, law-abiding men doing their duty as they saw it. He couldn't take the risk of dry-gulching innocent men any more than he could endanger Compton and his expedition by leading these men there. Fargo needed information and saw no way of getting it without first collecting a bullet in the gut.

He decided he had to do something drastic. A quick look at the stars positioned him again, then he put the Ovaro into a dangerous gallop across Thunder Basin going north and west toward the distant river.

"I hear 'im! He's makin' a break for it!"

"Git 'im!" came the faint cry of triumph. The trio thought they had flushed him.

Fargo intended to make their lives a living hell real fast if they kept after him.

He stayed low and guided his horse ever northward, hoping he didn't cross any prairie-dog holes. If the Ovaro stumbled now, both of them were lost. His reckless flight proved successful because he left the more cautious gunmen behind. As the distance between them widened,

Fargo changed his horse's gait to get the most from the powerful stallion that he could.

After what seemed an eternity, Fargo saw what he so fervently sought. Thin spirals of smoke twisted into the still night and veiled the stars. He had reached the Sioux encampment near the Belle Fourche River.

"Steady, steady," Fargo said, patting his horse's neck. He slowed and then stopped to rest the horse. He wanted the Ovaro to be in as good a condition as possible for what he intended doing if the outlaws were still after him.

They were.

It took them almost a half hour to catch up, but they came on like some unstoppable force of nature. They were intent on Fargo's trail and did not catch the smoke rising from half-a-hundred dying cooking fires in the Sioux encampment.

Fargo mounted and waited until the men spotted him. They broke into a ragged gallop, their horses tired from the pursuit. His Ovaro was tired, also, but he had been able to give the stallion a half hour to rest. Fargo bided his time until the stallion began to paw nervously at the ground, the approaching horsemen spooking it.

Only when he was sure they could not break off their pursuit did Fargo put his heels to his horse's flanks and let out a loud yell.

He rocketed forward and over one of the rolling hills to head down into the Sioux camp. The commotion caused a ripple throughout the village of tepees.

Fargo's horse trampled dying fires, and he kicked out at a Sioux brave who poked his head from his tepee. He cut to the left and rode through the outer edge of the camp, letting his horse carry him away from the agitated Indians.

Behind, Fargo heard rifles crack and the more distinctive sounds of six-guns firing. The three men had blundered into the camp as he had hoped. Fargo had gone into the camp and out before the Sioux were aware of what was happening. They would see the three outlaws and go after them rather than coming after him.

If the trio was lucky, they could get away before the Sioux mounted and came after them.

If they weren't lucky, that was the penalty they paid for dogging the Trailsman all night long.

Fargo got his bearings again and started back for Compton's camp.

9

Fargo approached Compton's camp cautiously. He had not avoided the three gunmen and an entire village of enraged Sioux to get himself shot by a nervous Paul Hancock. Somehow, he thought that if he came into Justin Compton's sights, he would not be shot unless the man wanted to bring him down like he had the buffalo.

"Hallo!" Fargo called. He rode slowly, hoping everyone could identify him; the morning sunlight warm on his face. The smell of cooking buffalo steak made his mouth water. Pierre was hard at work for his master.

The chef glared at Fargo as he dismounted.

"You kick up the dirt. It is all over my food," the chef said sullenly.

"Sorry about that," Fargo said. "I've always thought that everyone had to eat a peck of dirt before they died."

"For you, the dirt would make the food taste better. In my hands, I am the master chef and create masterpieces! You ruin it all."

"Don't be so hard on him, Pierre," Melissa said, hurrying up from where she had been working at the rear of the wagon. Her hands were white with flour, and she wore an apron that did nothing to hide the surge of her breasts.

"Where's Paul? I want a word with him."

"What's wrong, Skye? You were gone so long. I was worried." She came over, reached out, and stopped herself before she branded him with a floury handprint.

"No need," he said lightly. "I didn't run into anything I couldn't handle."

"But there's something that threatens us, isn't there?"

she pressed. The woman pushed a strand of black hair from her eyes, turning it white. Melissa looked flustered. "I wasn't imagining those men out there, was I?"

"No, you weren't," he told her.

"I'll get Paul. And Mr. Compton."

"Wait," Fargo said, grabbing her arm and holding her back. "I want to talk privately with you and your brother first."

"What you've learned will be of interest to Justin," she said, her blue eyes fixed on his. "Oh. I understand." She looked more frightened than flustered now and rushed off to fetch Paul.

Fargo took a deep, appreciative sniff of the steaks cooking, got a sneer from Pierre, and then decided food could wait until he'd spoken his piece. He walked a distance from camp and found a low rock to sit on while he waited. Melissa and Paul came over within a few minutes. By then Fargo had everything straight in his mind.

"You've banged into a real wasps' nest here," Fargo said. He quickly told them what he had seen of the five gunmen and the way he had riled the entire Sioux village to get away. "This means nothing but trouble you can't handle. Nobody can."

"What are we supposed to do?" asked Paul. "This is terrible danger we're in." Paul looked at his sister, but Fargo thought the man was worrying more about his own hide.

"I'll see you across the basin and to somewhere safe. Going north is dangerous since you'd run into the Sioux. The same might happen going west toward Fort Bridger. And it's a powerful long way to anywhere important if you go south."

"The outlaws that chased you were to the south," Paul said. "We can pack the wagons and head east right away."

"No." Melissa crossed her arms over her chest as her expression hardened. Fargo didn't like the look of it. She had come to a decision and it didn't match what was safe—or right.

"Unless you know who those men are, I'd say your brother's got the right idea," Fargo said.

"I have no idea who they might be, but we cannot turn and run. That's so . . . so cowardly."

"There's a big difference between being prudent and being a coward," Fargo pointed out. "We don't know what we're up against with the five men tagging along behind. But I do know what would happen if we cross the Sioux."

"Justin won't like it," Melissa said. "He wants to go to the river and do some fishing. I don't know what he is looking for. Trout, bass, something."

"He has his buffalo. Let him go home content with that. It mounts a danged sight better than a fish would," Fargo said. His words fell on an uneasy silence, making him realize there was more to Melissa's insistence on continuing than she had said. He asked.

"Skye, please." Melissa looked around, a touch of fear in her eyes now. "Justin won't pay us unless we deliver the goods. Paul and I are in desperate need of the money."

"That's it? That's the only reason you'd risk losing your scalp or getting shot in the back? Money?"

"You don't understand what it's like having money and then . . . not having any," she finished lamely. "We aren't like you. We don't have any real skills."

"You can read and cipher. That ought to get either of you—both of you jobs."

"Why ignore Justin and what he's offered us to guide him? Oh, Skye, this is about more than the money. If Paul and I can give him what he wants, it means we're not complete failures in life. We'll have *done* something."

Fargo took a deep breath and let it out slowly. He couldn't say he understood Melissa's motivations, but he was clear on one detail. She meant to stay with Compton. He knew arguing with her about what she was likely to accomplish was pointless. He could tell from the way her jaw was set and the determination in her shoulders.

"I'm going to talk to Compton," Fargo said. "If I can get him to return, he'd still pay you."

"Don't," Melissa said. "Don't rock the boat. We can tough this out, with or without you. I hope it is with you, Skye, but if it isn't, if you want to leave, I won't think any worse of you for going."

"She's right, Fargo," Paul said with some trepidation. "Mr. Compton's not gong to agree to quit until he's satisfied."

"I hope he'll be satisfied getting you all killed," Fargo said. If he had a brain in his head, he would ride off now. But he couldn't because it wasn't right. He had helped the Hancocks because they needed it—and they still did.

If he let them continue to act as guides and scouts for Justin Compton, he might be dooming them all.

"I'm still going to talk to Compton," Fargo said. He headed for the campfire where Pierre flopped one of the succulent buffalo steaks onto a platter and handed it to Compton.

"I want a word with you," Fargo said.

"Ah, Mr. Fargo. Have some of Pierre's exquisite victuals. That is what you could call this, isn't it? Victuals?" Compton inhaled the aroma of the steak and smacked his lips.

"The Sioux are all stirred up and—"

"I would like to go gold mining. Perhaps panning for some of the precious metal, since that seems more adventuresome than grubbing about like some kind of gopher in a mine shaft." Compton daintily used a small knife with a sharp blade to slice off a piece of the steak. He popped it into his mouth and chewed.

"There's no gold here," Fargo said. "This is the middle of Thunder Basin. What rocks there are you sit on, not mine." He saw his words did not penetrate. Fargo spoke now as if explaining to a small, willful child. "This is prairie. A grassland with buffalo herds."

"Yes, yes, I know that. I've bagged my buffalos. I need a new challenge, and what better than to hunt for gold?"

Fargo hesitated a moment as he thought over what Compton was saying. He saw a way of getting the expedition off the prairie and safely away from the Sioux while satisfying Compton's need for gold mining.

"Mountains are where you'd be most likely to find gold," Fargo said.

"Those Black Hills to the north, do you think?"

"Not those. Everyone knows there's no gold there," Fargo said, although he had heard rumors for years about small strikes. The white prospectors there might even be part of what riled up the Sioux. He wanted to steer Compton away from the river and the Sioux encampment and get him moving to the southwest. They would skirt the other Sioux camp. If Fargo read the signs right, the Sioux were all moving north. This would let Compton slip past, behind the Indians, as Fargo led him to the Laramie Mountains. There wasn't much along the way to slow them down. Fargo had heard rumors that Louis Guinard was building Fort Caspar, along with a trading post and bridge across the Platte, but Fargo knew a better ford to the east that would get them directly into the foothills of the Laramies.

"You are the frontiersman, sir," Compton said, as complacent as could be. He smacked his lips and continued eating his buffalo steak as Fargo went to make plans with Paul and Melissa. Somehow, the prospect of being on the trail a while longer with the beautiful woman struck him as the only good thing about the excursion south.

"I don't know, Fargo," Paul said, rubbing his hands against his pants legs. "That river looks mighty deep. You think we could, uh, pan for gold on this side?"

"The Platte doesn't have gold in it. Never even heard a whisper of a rumor about it. No, if Compton's going to find gold, it'll be yonder." Fargo pointed to the haze-cloaked Laramie Mountains on the far side of the river. He had no real hope that Compton would find anything there, either, but sometimes luck needed a helping hand.

Fargo knew enough about minerals to find fool's gold. A few sparkling, strategically placed pieces might be enough to satisfy Compton's irrational need to experience everything of the West on a single trip. He looked back to where the man scribbled furiously in his notebook, occasionally looking up, using his pencil to gauge distances and then returning to the avid writing.

John Frémont had made quite a name for himself traveling through this part of the country. Perhaps Justin Compton thought to duplicate the task. This brought a small smile to Fargo's lips. Kit Carson, Frémont's famous guide, had gained a reputation that reached all the way back to the Atlantic Ocean after Frémont's articles were printed. Somehow, Fargo doubted he would be elevated to a similar pinnacle of acclaim. Compton had the air of a man who hogged everything.

"If you'll look, you'll see the water's not as deep here," Fargo said, pointing to the ford across the Platte. It was almost a quarter mile to the other side, but he had made certain the wagons were properly sealed with both tarps and whatever sticky substances he could find in the supplies. He had hoped for tar but had disgusted Pierre by using molasses. The molasses would dissolve unless they made their way across the river quickly, but it only had to hold out the water for an hour or two.

"I can't see the bottom," Paul complained.

"We're going to float the wagons," Melissa said. "Skye explained that. The horses can swim and pull the wagons, if they are buoyant enough."

"I've done this before," Fargo assured the nervous man. Melissa tried to soothe her brother's worry but did not succeed. "Everyone ready for the crossing?" He looked at Compton, who tucked his notebook and papers into a pouch, sealed it, and then wrapped it all in oilskin.

"I say, Mr. Fargo, this is a great adventure. Let's go!"

Fargo checked with Bruno and Charles, saw the determination on their faces and knew they wouldn't panic. He turned his Ovaro to the swiftly flowing river. He judged their entry point and where they would be swept as they crossed. The spot on the other side of the river was smooth and could serve as a rest area once they had gotten to safety.

His stallion pranced about, eager to get the watery trek over. Fargo gave the horse its head and plunged into the icy river. It took away his breath for a moment, then every bit of his concentration went to guiding the Ovaro across. He glanced behind at the wagons and saw the drivers were dutifully working the reins to keep the teams pulling. Now and then a hoof might touch a rocky bottom, but mostly the horses had to pull the bobbing wagons across through swimming alone.

"This isn't going to work," Fargo heard Paul mutter from somewhere behind. Melissa snapped something at her brother Fargo didn't catch, but it quieted him until they reached the south bank of the Platte.

Fargo's horse struggled out of the river and shook itself like a dog to get the water off. Turning in the saddle, Fargo watched as the wagons came across without any problem. Bruno and Charles were soon on the riverbank beside Fargo.

"Come on!" Fargo called to Melissa and Paul. The two had let their horses go with the flow rather than cutting across it and were going to come onto land farther east. He rode along the river shouting encouragement to them. When they both reached dry land, Fargo heaved a sigh of relief. He had not been looking forward to diving into the swiftly flowing, cold river to pull out either of them.

"Where's Justin?" asked Melissa anxiously. "He was behind us, and I lost sight of him halfway across."

"Hello!" came the hearty shout. "Up here!"

Compton sat astride his horse on a rocky butte. The man took off his now bedraggled hat and waved it in a circle over his head and let out a shout of glee.

"How'd he get up there?" wondered Paul.

"He came ashore sooner than you," Fargo said. He picked out the most likely path to the top of the butte but saw no reason to follow it to join Compton. Their route into the Laramie Mountains was lower, off the riverbank and directly south from this point.

"Do you need to scout from there, Skye?" asked Melissa, her expression flushed. He wasn't sure exactly what she was asking. It seemed she wanted to join Compton in looking down on the river and the grasslands they had just crossed but didn't want to ride up the trail by herself.

"I know the lay of the land already," Fargo said. The crestfallen look on her face told him how much she had wanted to stand on the hill with Compton and share his triumph.

"Very well," she said softly, but as the dark-haired woman rode off she cast several backward glances in the direction of the butte.

Fargo insisted on examining the wagons to be sure they were still intact. Pierre griped about him poking through the supplies to see if water had ruined anything, and the two drivers appeared caught up in the gold fever that already infected their employer. Fargo was finally satisfied the wagons were in good enough shape to continue. By the time they rolled, Compton had come down from the hilltop and joined them.

"That was exciting, Mr. Fargo. I can hardly wait to see what new adventures lie ahead," Compton said with gusto. He sucked in a deep breath and pounded his chest. "This land makes a soul come alive. I can understand why you live here."

"It's wide-open," Fargo said. "Are you thinking of moving out here?"

"I?" Compton laughed. "Hardly. Leaving the parlors of high society in New York would be a true loss I could not bear, but traveling through this land *is* invigorating."

Fargo heard something more in Compton's words but did not pursue it. He yelled to Bruno and got the driver onto a double-rutted track leading south.

"Who else has been along here?" asked Paul, seeing how exactly the wagons' wheels fit the ruts in the dirt. "This looks like a well-traveled route."

"Not so many come this way anymore," Fargo said. "Most are on the Oregon Trail, going through South Pass."

"You mentioned a fort being built," said Melissa. "Should we stop there for supplies?"

"There's no need. Compton has plenty for another month on the trail." Fargo found himself constantly astounded at the wide variety of foodstuffs Compton had brought along. The man ate high on the hog every night and never seemed to deplete his larder. The buffalo meat had only extended it, and Fargo knew there was plenty for all of them for the rest of Compton's excursion.

"All right," she said. "I had hoped to meet other people."

Fargo laughed. "What's wrong? The folks you see around you aren't good enough?"

"Oh, Skye, that's not what I meant." She reached over and laid her hand on his arm. He felt an electric tingle at her touch. "It gets lonely out here. I am not cut out to be a frontier wife."

Fargo saw that. Her brother wasn't pioneer material, either. The two of them were hothouse flowers that had been uprooted with the promise of a better life after a temporary transplanting.

"He's quite a piece of work," Fargo said, staring at Compton as the man rode along taking in every detail of the land.

"That he is," Melissa said.

Before she could say another word, a crack as loud as any gunshot spooked their horses.

"Take cover!" shouted Paul. "We're being attacked. It's the Indians!"

"Wait, no!" Fargo held up his hand to stop Bruno from whipping his team into a trot.

"What happened?" asked Compton, galloping back from his position in front of their small wagon train. "I heard a shot."

"Not a shot. Look," Fargo said. The wagon Charles drove canted at a crazy angle. The driver had been pitched out and sat in the dirt, stunned but unharmed. "The front axle broke."

"What bad luck," Compton said. "Can you fix it?"

"You didn't bring any spare axles," Fargo said, knowing their inventory well, "and I doubt you can fix it with a loaf of Pierre's bread."

The chef climbed from the bed of the broken-down wagon and glared at Fargo.

"You'll need a long straight piece of wood at least five feet long. That'll give enough leeway to whittle it down so it's as true as we can make it."

"That sounds as if it will take a long time," Compton said. "I see trees, but they are miles away."

"Pitch camp," Fargo ordered Bruno, Charles, and the other servants. "We're going to be here for a spell."

"Bruno, you know something of woodworking," Compton said. "Deal with the matter. Mr. Fargo and I are going to find gold. Come along, sir. The gold in them thar hills is waitin' for us!"

Compton let out another shout of pure joy and galloped off in a cloud of dust.

Fargo found himself torn between helping fix the wagon and keeping Compton out of trouble. He glanced at Melissa and saw the answer in her eyes. He put his heels to the Ovaro's flanks and lit out after Compton, trusting that Bruno and the others could do a competent enough job on the wagon axle to get moving again in a few days.

Until then, he got to watch Justin Compton search for gold.

10

"Please, Skye, don't argue. Paul explained why we have to do this."

"It's dangerous being away from the wagons," Fargo told Melissa. She looked as if she was going to break into tears at any moment, but he was the only one who noticed. Paul and Compton rode ahead, chatting as if they didn't have a care in the world. Fargo worried about how Compton's men would repair the wagon and when they would be able to come along.

Now he had Melissa and Paul to worry about, too.

"He won't think any less of you if you go back to the wagons," Fargo said.

"We're supposed to be his *guides*," the pretty woman insisted. "If we deserted him again, he would think poorly of us."

"And not pay you?" Fargo asked sharply.

"Yes," she replied, equally sharp. "All Justin talks of is how you led him to the buffalo herd and how he bagged that damned woolly monster. Paul and I need his money, Skye."

"I'm not trying to cut you out." Fargo could not explain it any better than that. He had not even wanted to come along, but she had appealed to his sense of honor. After seeing how easy it was for her brother—and Compton—to get into trouble they never anticipated, Fargo had felt an obligation to both the woman and her wards. Fargo laughed ruefully. It was almost as if Melissa was Paul's mother and had him tied to her apron strings. She was, without doubt, the one in that family who took charge.

That didn't make Fargo any less inclined to help. She needed his assistance as much as Paul.

"Did you spot the riders again?" he asked suddenly. Melissa's blue eyes went wide with shock. She opened her mouth, but nothing came out for a moment. Then she hastily shook her head.

She was lying, and he thought he knew why. The gunmen were the perfect reason to call off the expedition. Compton had no desire to tangle with them. He might enjoy the notion of seeing an "aboriginal" Sioux or shooting a buffalo, but even an rich man's son from New York understood how desperate and dangerous a potential robber could be.

"You're paid for the time you're out here, aren't you? The longer you and your brother keep Compton out West, the more money you stand to collect."

"That's part of it, Skye," she said. She stared directly at him as she spoke, and he knew this would be the truth. "We make more, yes, but I am not the kind who cheats a customer. Justin is paying good money for this trip and the more we can deliver, the more generous he will be—and the better I will feel about what Paul and I have done for him."

"It's one thing to take pride in a job well done," Fargo said, "but it's another to get yourself killed doing it when it really doesn't matter."

"You think we're out of our league leading this excursion. You're not too far wrong in that, Skye, but we've done all right. Not as good as you could do, but we've done all right."

"I'm most worried about the five owlhoots dogging our tracks," Fargo said. "Why are they so persistent? Who are they?"

"I don't know, I don't know!" Melissa's voice turned shrill with strain. "Keep an eye peeled for them, Skye. That's all I can say."

Fargo and Melissa rode side by side until they reached the spot where Compton had halted. He stared up a steep trail leading into the foothills.

"What do you think, Mr. Fargo? Is this gold-bearing rock?" Justin asked.

"That's hard to tell without blasting." Fargo said. "There's a small stream making its way down from above. That might be the spot to try your hand at panning. The water washes gold flecks along the stream and deposits them on the shore."

"An excellent idea. There are trees for shelter and an adequate spot to pitch camp for the night. I can hardly wait to get started."

"Paul can show you how to slosh the water around just right to get the gold to settle," Fargo said. "I ought to do some scouting to be sure this is the best place."

Melissa shot him a frightened look. "Can I come along?" she asked. "They'll be busy panning and—"

"Oh, certainly, Miss Hancock," Compton said. "Your brother and I will be deeply engrossed in this until later, when you can begin preparations for our supper."

Compton and Paul went off to begin their work on the stream.

"Is there any chance of them finding gold?" Melissa asked. She licked her lips nervously. Finding gold was the farthest thing from her mind.

"I doubt there's anything here, but fool's gold sparkles real pretty. That might be enough for Compton." He saw how distraught she had become. "Why did you want to come with me?"

"Safety," she said. "I did see the riders. You had started across the Platte. Paul and I entered the water and I looked back to see how the wagons were faring. Up on a hill some distance away I spotted two of them."

Fargo knew she could not say positively these two belonged to the gang he had tangled with earlier. He couldn't identify the men since he had never gotten a good look at any of them. He had overheard a few names being called out, but those were as liquid as the water flowing between the banks of the Platte. Men in this part of the country all too often sported false names. Some were running from the law. Others ran from themselves.

And it was not out of the question that these men were the ones who had shot at him. Looking for a good ford across the raging Platte River occupied most pilgrims.

"Thanks for letting me know you *did* see something."

"I should have told you sooner. You might have caught them when they crossed the river."

"There might be nothing to worry about," Fargo assured her, but he wondered. His gut instinct told him the men Melissa had seen were part of the gang since they hadn't come down to cross with the wagons. The more people risking such a dangerous trip, the better everyone's chance was.

If the five had any sense, they would have waited until the wagons were out of sight before starting. He would not have been in any position to stop all five, unless he wanted to potshot them as they struggled in the swift river. It wasn't Fargo's style to ambush anyone like that, even these mysterious, gun-toting strangers.

"Do you think they'll be all right?" Melissa asked.

"Compton and your brother? They'll be fine. I'm more worried about getting the wagon axle repaired."

"I've talked with Bruno. He is quite handy," Melissa said. She looked at him and smiled, looking more relaxed than she had in some time. "Like you."

Fargo urged his horse up the final slope of a rocky hill and looked around. From this angle he could see the wagons but not Compton or Paul. That suited him fine. Bruno, Charles, and the others appeared to be working diligently. In the distance roared the Platte and behind him trotted Melissa.

He dismounted as she did. For a moment they looked only at one another. Words weren't what they wanted now that they were alone. They flowed into each other's arms and Fargo kissed Melissa. Hard. She returned the kiss with equal passion as he pulled her lush body to his.

He felt the crush of her firm breasts and the beating of her heart. When he broke off the deep kiss, they were both out of breath.

"I want you, Skye," she said in a low, husky voice.

He reluctantly released her. The woman slipped from him and waited as he untied his bedroll from behind his saddle. He found a spot that didn't look too rocky and spread out his blanket. Melissa dropped to her knees and began unbuttoning her blouse. From his position above her Fargo saw the milky globes of her breasts slowly revealed. Every new glimpse of her made him a little harder.

"Your turn, Skye," she said as she tossed aside her blouse. Melissa was bare to the waist. Her breasts bobbed delightfully, capped with cherry-red nipples. The breeze blowing across the butte caused them to harden— or was it lust?

Fargo didn't care. The sight of the alluring woman was enough to make him hurry in dropping his gun belt and shucking off his own shirt. Melissa came closer and reached up, her hands stroking over his chest.

"So big, so strong," she murmured. "And so hard!"

The dark-haired vixen unfastened the buttons of his fly and let his manhood leap out like a horse taking a barrier. She stroked up and down its rigid length and then popped the tip into her mouth. Fargo went weak in the knees when her eager tongue began swirling about to stimulate him completely.

She ran her nimble fingers all over his crotch. Then she began bobbing back and forth, taking more and more of him into her mouth, cradling him with her mouth, cradling him with her tongue and then retreating until only the tip of his manhood remained in her lips.

Melissa looked up at him, blue eyes dancing with lust. Fargo reached down and ran his fingers through her long, dark locks and began guiding her in a rhythm that achieved the impossible. She excited him even more.

"That's enough," Fargo said. "I want to give you as much a thrill as you're giving me."

Melissa let him slip from her mouth. She smiled up at him and said, "I'm enjoying this. A lot."

"You'll like this a whale of a lot more," Fargo said, dropping to his knees taking her in his arms again. They sank back as they kissed, Melissa pinned under his weight. She struggled a little and finally got her skirts positioned right. The portion of his anatomy that had been in her mouth now sought a different entrance to her trembling body.

He found it. He parted the woman's nether lips and then drove forward until he was fully within her. Fargo paused then, relishing the feel of the tightness surrounding him. A twitch of his hips caused Melissa to cry out.

"Am I hurting you?" he asked.

"No, no, I can't control myself. You fill me up so, Skye."

He smiled as he levered himself up on his arms so he could look down into her face. Melissa's eyes were closed and she bit her lower lip. He pulled back slightly and produced the response he had hoped for. Melissa moaned softly and lifted her buttocks off the blanket and tried to ram herself fully around his manhood again.

Fargo didn't let her. He wanted to build the excitement in her until she felt the way he did. A small rotation of his hips stirred him around in her most intimate passage before he drew back all the way.

"No, don't, Skye. Don't tease me. I want it hard! Fast and hard!"

"Like this?"

His hips slammed forward and lifted her off the ground again. This time Melissa cried out in joy and clutched fiercely at him. He felt her fingernails cutting into his arms and shoulders. The pain was nothing compared to the sensations mounting in his loins. He felt as if a prairie fire had started. Burning with need, he shot forward like a locomotive piston. Fargo began grinding his crotch into Melissa's, awakening all the hidden desires in the woman's slender, supple body.

He withdrew and then began the age-old rhythm of a man loving a woman. Every thrust produced a new cry of delight from Melissa's lips. Fargo enjoyed the sight of her passion-racked face, the way her breasts danced about, the feel of her body around and against his, everything about their coupling.

Faster and faster he stroked, their bodies striving to

exact the maximum pleasure from one another. Sweat beaded Fargo's forehead as he thrust and felt the heat building within his body. When Melissa's gasped, arched her back, and cried out in release, he almost lost control. Her tight female sheath clamped fiercely around him, but Fargo fought to contain himself. There would be even more, even better sensations to come.

"Yes, Skye, more. Give it all to me."

Melissa tensed and relaxed her strong inner muscles. He picked up the pace and the heat of friction burned at his resolve until the white-hot tides locked within him had to be released.

The sound of Melissa gasping out in ecstasy once again set him off. He slammed forward as if trying to split her body in half as he spilled his seed. Locked together, reacting as one, they clung to each other until the winds of desire died down and only the softer summer wind whipping across the hill remained.

He sank down and lay beside her. For a long time they said nothing. There was nothing to say.

"I wish there could be more, Skye," Melissa finally said.

"More? You'll wear me out!"

"No, not that. That was fine. More than fine. It was wonderful, the best," she said, almost babbling. "I meant more between us. You'd never be happy in a place like St. Louis, would you?"

"You'd never be happy out West," Fargo said, finishing her thought for her. "That doesn't mean we shouldn't enjoy what we have right now."

"No, it doesn't." Melissa giggled like a schoolgirl. "And I certainly *did* enjoy it." She reached down and found his limp length. "I'd enjoy a bit more."

"You're getting greedy," Fargo said. "We should head back before Compton comes looking for us."

"Or Paul. He can be so protective," Melissa said. The resignation in her voice told Fargo she had it all wrong. She thought he looked after her. Everything Fargo had seen showed it was the other way around. Melissa was the one who took care of her inept brother.

Fargo disengaged from Melissa's arms and sat up. He got into his pants and put on his shirt. Watching the good-looking woman dress intrigued him, but he afforded her some privacy. Fargo got to his feet and grabbed his gun belt. As he strapped on the Colt, he walked to the edge of the butte and looked back toward the wagons.

Nothing had changed.

Fargo scanned the horizon and saw a storm building across Thunder Basin. That would reduce the threat of another prairie fire, but it would blow down on them and make their lives miserable for a day or two. Traveling in mud with a shoddily repaired wagon axle did not appeal to Fargo.

He continued his examination of the countryside and stopped when he looked directly east. Shielding his eyes, Fargo got a better look and saw a small dust cloud caused by horses galloping. He waited a few seconds and determined the riders were heading in his direction.

Sioux? Possibly, though most of them were farther north. If the riders Melissa had seen on the other side of the Platte had crossed at the next ford, they might have come out far enough east to be riding along that trail.

"Come on," Fargo said, cinching down his gun belt. "We shouldn't leave Compton and your brother alone too long."

Melissa sighed and nodded. She finished buttoning her blouse and stood, smoothing out wrinkles in her dress.

"Let's go, Skye," she said, smiling at him. "The sooner we get them tended to, the sooner we can . . . go scouting again."

Fargo wasn't going to argue. He only hoped that the riders didn't bring so much trouble down on their necks that he and Melissa wouldn't get a chance for another "scout."

11

Neither Paul nor Compton noticed how Fargo kept looking around. He had not told them or Melissa about the riders coming their way because there was no need to worry them, but he was getting antsy about their wagons. Bruno, Charles, and the other servants should be warned that they might be attacked since the wagons were a more likely target for outlaws than Compton and those with him.

Or were they?

"You finding enough gold?" asked Fargo, peering down where Paul knelt in the stream. His pants were wet and parts of his shirt turned dark with water. He looked thoroughly uncomfortable but said nothing.

"Not a speck of gold, Mr. Fargo. This is not a good stream. Perhaps we should try another," Justin Compton said from his vantage point on the nearby rock. He was dry. He had let Paul do all the work sloshing water around in the pan, trying to get rid of dross and leaving only color.

If Paul had seen even a glint, he would have called Compton down and let him finish the work. That Compton was as dry as a bone told Fargo how poorly the hunt had gone so far.

"Let's get back to the wagons. We can bring them up once the axle is repaired and do a thorough search for a good spot," Fargo said.

"No!" cried Compton, jumping to his feet. He slapped his thigh and produced a snap that was close enough to a gunshot that Fargo jumped, his hand going for the Colt at his belt. Neither Compton nor Paul noticed how restless he was. Melissa did. Her blue eyes widened at his move for his six-gun, but she said nothing.

"It's not good letting Bruno work all by himself," Fargo said, trying to find an argument Compton would go for that didn't require coming out and telling what he had seen from the hilltop. Fargo might be wrong about the riders, and crying wolf would jeopardize his credibility with Compton. From the way Compton seemed to be a lightning rod for trouble. Fargo knew one bad call on his part might doom Compton, his servants, and Melissa and her brother later.

"He's competent to do the work without my supervision," Compton said. "I feel we are close to gold here. Is there another stream to mine?"

"To pan," Paul grumbled.

"It'll be here tomorrow, and you can have the full comfort of everything in your wagons," Fargo said, angling for another argument that might appeal to Compton. He had not counted on the gold fever being so strong in the man.

"Hang it all! I want to continue. I shall do so, with or without you, Mr. Fargo. I value your expertise in such matters, but others have found gold without it."

"I can go back to see how the repairs are coming," Melissa said. "If they're done, I can bring them back here."

"No," Fargo said, sharper than he intended. Letting the dark-haired woman ride alone in the direction of the unknown men—who might well be the outlaws Fargo had fought—put her into danger. "Stay here. We can finish up soon. Before sundown, so we can get back to the wagons."

"Have you become so attached to the luxuries of my larder, Mr. Fargo? Who would have thought it?" Compton laughed, gesturing to Paul to mount and head up into the foothills so they could hunt for gold at a better location.

As Paul and her employer rode ahead, Melissa hung back with Fargo.

"What's wrong, Skye? You're acting strangely."

He considered dancing around what he suspected, then decided she deserved to know. Compton and Paul did, too, but Fargo doubted anything short of the entire Sioux nation would deter the rich man from his gold hunt.

"When we were on the hill," he said, choosing his words carefully, "after we had finished and you were dressing, I spotted men coming in this direction." He explained how they might be the same riders that Melissa had seen back at the river and how they could have forded the Platte at a different spot.

"But you don't know?"

"I can't know unless I talk to them," Fargo admitted. "This part of Wyoming seems awfully crowded right now—unless we're running into the same five outlaws over and over."

"If they are road agents, why don't they just rob us? Or try?" she asked.

Fargo wasn't sure he had a good answer to that. Compton's expedition was large enough to give even a five-man gang a run for their money, but an ambush, a quick stickup, and the robbery would be over. Highwaymen robbed stagecoaches with armed guards all the time. This made Fargo think there was something more than mere robbery keeping the five men on their trail.

"Is Compton carrying anything that's really valuable?" he asked.

"Not that I know of," she said, frowning.

Fargo had no reason to doubt Melissa and Paul when they told him that they were as poor as church mice. The servants had nothing not provided them by Compton. The wagons, the tack, the food, and other supplies were all valuable but not to the point of interesting a gang of highwaymen. There wasn't any cash or gold that could be carried off easily, and Fargo couldn't see an ill-disciplined gang following this long to steal fancy food. If they got the expensive provender along with gold, they would devour it, but never in a hundred years would they trail the expedition this long unless there was a monetary payoff.

"No jewels or gold? Anything like that?"

"Nothing," she assured him, and he believed her.

"We ought to return to camp so everyone's able to watch everyone else's back," Fargo said.

"Oh, really?" Melissa said. "Is that the way it is? You want everyone else to ogle my backside when you're the only one I want doing it?"

Fargo had to laugh. "There's safety in numbers. If the entire party sticks together, I can go ask the gents what brought them into Wyoming and put them on our trail without worrying about you. So it's best for you to sit on that rump of yours and save it for me."

"That's better," she said. Melissa sobered, thought a moment on what Fargo meant about him riding out to confront the riders. "You going alone to spy on them is mighty dangerous," Melissa said. "I can sit on my backside, but I wouldn't want you getting yours blown off."

"Talking to them is the only way I know to find out if we have trouble brewing. There might be a reason for them to be riding around—and being so nervy."

"You can leave Paul and me with Justin so you could—"

"No." Fargo's flat statement cut off Melissa's words.

She looked sharply at him. Her lips thinned, and he saw determination coming into her posture as her shoulders squared and her jaw tensed.

"We saw to Justin fine before you showed up. We can do it again right now."

"There's safety in numbers. Besides," Fargo pointed out, "your brother's not very good with a rifle." He stopped short of passing judgment on Compton's marksmanship. He still had not figured out if the man was very good or very lucky.

"Fargo, up here! Come look!" Paul Hancock called from higher on the hillside. "We might have something."

"Don't say anything about the riders," Fargo said. Melissa was mad at him now for impugning her skills and turned a cold shoulder as she rode ahead. Fargo followed, craning around to see if he could locate the men on their heels. The back trail was as empty as a whore's soul.

"See, Fargo? What do you make of this?" called Paul, jumping around like he had sat on an anthill.

Fargo dismounted and went to the small pool fed by a waterfall from higher on the mountain. This was a good watering spot for his horse, but he wasn't sure it was good for finding gold.

"See? At the bottom of the waterfall. The water's brought gold down from above. This *is* gold, isn't it?" Paul bubbled over with excitement at his find.

Fargo took the knife Paul held out. Tiny golden specks glinted on the blade where Paul had lifted them out of the water. Fargo examined the tiny flecks carefully, then handed the knife back.

"Looks to be gold," Fargo said. "I'm no expert, and it usually takes an assay to prove the claim, but you might have hit on a good one." He looked around, then asked, "Where's Compton?"

"Don't worry about him," Paul said. "He wanted to see what the top of the waterfall looked like. He thought there might be nuggets caught up there on the lip above this pool."

Fargo shot a look at Melissa, then took off at a run to find the way to the top of the waterfall. The water cascaded down almost thirty feet into the pool where Paul had found the gold flakes. Finding a path to the top was difficult. Scrambling for purchase alongside the waterfall, Fargo scaled the rocks on the far side of the pool, got to a ledge halfway up, then inched along it until he could grip a rock higher up. He wondered if Compton had come this way; then he saw signs that someone had done so. If it was Compton, he had to be part mountain goat.

A daring jump afforded Fargo a handgrip. He pulled himself up until his boots found purchase. Then the climb to the top was easier. He flopped over the top onto a small level area. The stream had cut a deep channel in solid rock, leaving behind very little gravel as it sped to the brink and tumbled to the pool below.

"Compton!" shouted Fargo. "Where are you?" He rested his hand on the butt of his Colt, fearing the worst when he didn't get an immediate response. Fargo went to the stream, hunting for Compton's tracks, but the rocky ground wasn't right for leaving footprints. He walked quickly upstream, alert for trouble.

The crunch of gravel under a boot sole set Fargo into motion. He whipped out his six-shooter and cocked it as he swung around. A startled Justin Compton stood behind him.

"Don't shoot, Mr. Fargo! You can have the gold."

"Are you all right?" Fargo demanded.

"Why, yes, except you pointing that smoke wagon at me. That is what you gunfighters call it, isn't it? A smoke wagon?"

Fargo relaxed, let the hammer down on his six-gun and returned it to his holster.

"Why didn't you answer when I called out?"

"I was, uh, answering a call of nature behind those bushes. It did not seem a good time to draw attention to myself."

"Then you came out after I passed?"

"I say, Mr. Fargo, you are snippy. Is it because we found gold without your assistance? Don't feel that way. I value you highly."

"Did you find any more up here?"

"Not a speck," Compton admitted. "I had hoped to find a nugget or two. I have heard of some as large as a man's fist. That would have been a most excellent exhibit back in New York."

"A chunk of gold that large draws attention anywhere," Fargo said. He saw that, while Compton might have been relieving himself, there was more to his climb to this part of the mountain. His shirt was unbuttoned and his notebook poked out. When Compton realized Fargo was taking special notice of it, he hastily tucked it away and buttoned his shirt for safekeeping.

"Shall we return to the pool where the doughty Mr. Hancock is hard at work panning for more gold?"

"I saw what he found," Fargo said, "but I'm not a claim-jumper."

"A thousand pardons if I might have insinuated that

you were," Compton said. The man returned to where the stream fell into the pool, looked over, then waved to Melissa and Paul. "It's a shame the water is not deeper. A dive from here would be exhilarating."

Fargo thought it was close to suicidal, even if the water had been deep enough.

"Where did you come up?"

"There," Compton said, pointing out the route Fargo had also taken. "That was the easiest climb."

"You tried other places?" asked Fargo.

"Not at all. I looked up and saw how the rock afforded the best places for resting and climbing." Without any hesitation, Compton turned, got his feet down the slope, and slid away. Fargo grabbed for him but quickly saw there was no reason to help the man. Compton went down the stony face like a spider on a wall, finding the ledge where Fargo had made his way laterally and then down to the pool from there. Fargo followed more slowly, wondering if Compton was simply reckless or if he might be a better rock climber.

When Fargo reached the pool, Paul was shaking his head and speaking in a low voice with Compton.

"So there's no more, eh? That doesn't matter. I found my gold," Compton declared. "We can return to the wagons now."

Fargo shook his head in amazement. Only a couple hours earlier he couldn't pry Compton loose from his gold hunt. Now that he had a dollar or two of color, he was willing to give up.

"I looked, Mr. Compton," Paul said anxiously. "I hunted everywhere for a nugget or two. There might be more flakes of gold. I can pan it out if you want."

Compton was already mounted. He spoke cheerfully to Melissa, then got his horse started on the trail back down the mountainside.

"Thanks," Fargo said to Paul.

"What did I do?"

"You got him moving back to the wagons," Fargo said. He didn't explain further because there was no need to spook Paul. He didn't have the courage his sister did and telling him of the approaching riders would frighten him.

Paul hastily packed and mounted. "I'm glad I found the gold. It is real gold, isn't it, Fargo?"

"Probably. Fool's gold is usually embedded in quartz."

Fargo listened with half an ear as Paul rattled on how difficult it had been finding the gold in the pool and how he wished Compton had let him stay longer. When they reached the foothills and the land sloped down towards the wagons, Fargo turned wary. He swiveled around constantly as he sought a dust cloud or even a rider coming up on them from the east.

They reached the wagons without any danger presenting itself.

"How's the repair going?" Fargo asked Bruno. The man grunted and turned away.

"Come now, my good man. Answer Mr. Fargo. He has a right to know," Compton said.

"Found a tree. Green wood's gonna bend if I use it."

"There is hardly time to season the wood, now is there, Bruno?" asked Compton. "Use it. Cut several more likely axles so we can move on with the dawn."

"Are you returning to St. Louis?" Fargo asked.

"What? Why, of course not, Mr. Fargo. There are so many experiences to savor out West. I have bagged a buffalo and panned for gold. Now I want to break a mustang."

Bruno grumbled and went off when Pierre rang a dinner bell calling them to eat.

Fargo's belly growled, and he wanted to talk with Melissa as they ate. He had to decide what to do. Compton had promised him decent pay to scout, but he had yet to earn it. Fargo did not want to leave Melissa and Paul to their own devices, but Compton might extend his trip West interminably if he stuck around. Playing wet-nurse was not something Fargo relished.

"Come along now, everyone," Compton said cheerily. "Chow down. Pierre has outdone himself with this buffalo ragout. I doubt I will ever tire of it. Excellent, Pierre, simply superb!" Compton put his fingertips to his lips and made a loud smacking noise.

Paul stoked up the campfire as the sun sank and a

chill came to the foothills. He warmed his hands but still shivered.

"You are going to catch your death of cold, man," Compton said. "It must be all that sloshing around in mountain streams you did for me."

"Oh, here's your gold, sir," Paul said, taking out a white linen handkerchief and opening it. The firelight caused the flakes to sparkle, making Fargo believe Paul really had found gold.

"Thank you. I'll put this away with the rest of my mementos of the excursion." Compton tucked the handkerchief with the gold into his coat pocket. He hesitated as he looked at Paul. "You are shivering. A moment."

Compton went off. Fargo took the opportunity to sit beside Melissa, where Compton had been.

"I'll scout the riders," Fargo said. "If there's no danger, I'll move on. As much as I'd like to stay on, Compton doesn't show any sign of calling it quits."

"Do what you want," she said coldly.

Fargo wondered what irritated her. Before he could ask, Compton came back carrying a large box.

"Here, my boy. All yours. Go on, try it on."

Paul opened the box and saw a red velvet jacket with flashy gold braid on the sleeves.

"I had it made specially in London but have never found an occasion to wear it. Go on, try it."

"Thank you, Mr. Compton. This is very generous." Paul slipped into it. The jacket fit him well. He ran his hands over the velvet sleeves and smiled. "This is warm, too."

"Come over here so I can see what needs to be done. Charles can tailor it to your frame."

As Paul stepped around the campfire, a sharp crack split the quiet twilight. Paul stiffened, looked around, and then sank bonelessly to the ground.

"Paul!" cried Melissa, rushing to her brother. She cradled his head in her lap, oblivious to the blood leaking from his back and staining her dress.

Fargo pushed Compton to the ground and glared at him when he tried to get back to his feet. "Get under the wagon and stay there. Bruno, Charles, get your rifles. The rest of you," he shouted to the milling, frightened servants, "get under the wagon with Compton! Don't let anything happen to him."

Fargo grabbed his Henry and climbed into the driver's box of the closest wagon to get some elevation before returning fire. He judged that Paul had been shot in the back from the direction of a low hill to the east.

He hunted for any trace of the bushwhacker but saw nothing. The unseen killer had fired once with deadly accuracy, then vanished into the gathering darkness settling over the Wyoming mountains.

12

"Paul? Paul!" cried Melissa, hugging her brother to her as if her embrace would somehow cheat death. Tears ran down her cheeks. She was trembling and quickly losing control of her emotions. "It can't be. Please, not this way. Please!"

Fargo glanced at Justin Compton, who stood stunned on the other side of the campfire. The man slowly came out of his shock and hurried to Melissa, taking her in his arms and pulling her away.

"Come now, Melissa. There's nothing you can do for him, and we're all in danger. We shouldn't stay out in the open where we might be shot, too."

Fargo wasn't sure about that. The single shot had been sudden and completely unexpected. If the sniper intended to kill anyone else, he would have kept firing while surprise was on his side.

He looked at the dead Paul Hancock and wondered why the innocuous, naive young man had died. There was only one explanation: the fancy coat Compton had given him. From a distance in the twilight, all a bushwhacker could see was the bright gold glinting in the firelight and the brilliant crimson velvet material—a coat no one but Justin Compton was likely to wear.

That Paul had an enemy willing to gun him down was possible, but Fargo doubted it. Men died but not like this. Paul had to have died accidentally; Compton must have been the intended victim.

"Stay under cover and don't let the fire flare up," Fargo ordered. Pierre grumbled but went to kick dirt onto the flames. Fargo glanced at Compton sitting under a wagon, still holding a sobbing Melissa, and knew there was nothing he could do here. He picked up his tack and went to saddle his stallion. It was time to settle accounts.

Starting with Paul Hancock's killer.

The Ovaro protested and then settled down. The paint had been ridden hard the past week or so but was stouthearted and ready for any demand Fargo might put on it. He sheathed his rifle, mounted, and rode directly for the hill from where the killing bullet must have come.

Fargo rode in ravines and tried to follow the contours of the rugged land as he made his way inexorably toward the dark hill. Alert for any sign of movement, he got to the foot of the hill and dismounted. He pulled his Henry from the saddle sheath and jacked a round into the chamber before proceeding. Halfway up the hill, he turned to look at Compton's camp. The shot was a long one but not impossible. Pierre had done well keeping the fire down and restricting the light that might betray another target, but Fargo imagined he could make out Paul's body on the ground.

The red coat with gold braid couldn't have made the man a better target than if a bull's-eye had been drawn on his back.

Dropping to a crouch, Fargo listened for any movement. He heard small sounds, animals moving about, but nothing large enough to interest him. The few yards to the top of the hill were quickly covered, leaving him with an unrestricted view in a full circle. He lifted his rifle to his shoulder and aimed at one of Compton's wagons. It was an easier shot than he had thought before.

But Fargo could not make out anyone's face at this range. This reinforced his belief that Paul had been the unfortunate recipient of Compton's coat—and whatever curse followed the rich man across the Wyoming grasslands.

He dropped to his hands and knees to begin a thorough search of the area. It took him less than five minutes to find the spent brass from a rifle. He fancied he could still feel the heat from the slug leaving the neck, although it was pure imagination. The rock on the hill and the chilly night breeze had cooled the brass almost immediately as it was levered from the firing chamber.

Fargo backed off a few feet and studied a dirt patch. He found a distinct boot print with a large notch cut into the heel. The sides of the print were distinct, showing it was fresh. No matter how he scoured the area, though, he could not find any other prints. Giving up, he made his way down the side of the hill away from the camp. A fresh pile of horse dung, still warm, convinced Fargo he was on the right trail. Not ten feet away he found hoofprints in softer dirt.

He retrieved his Ovaro and got down to the serious job of overtaking Paul's killer.

He would be able to travel faster if he waited for dawn, but Fargo felt a gnawing need to bring Paul's killer to justice. More than that and what it would mean for Melissa, Fargo wanted answers. Justin Compton was a rich man's son on a lark across the Wyoming grasslands, but he drew trouble to him like flypaper. It showed up and then stuck tight until someone died.

Like Paul Hancock.

Fargo knew the young man had made his own decisions about escorting Compton, but an obligation remained not only to his sister but his memory. Compton had not needed Paul and Melissa to accompany him but had hired them anyway. Not once had Fargo seen an instance where Compton actually relied on Paul; to the contrary, he showed remarkable abilities. He could climb like a mountain goat, shoot with incredible accuracy, and even do a fair job butchering a carcass. Fargo would not have expected a city-born-and-bred dandy to have such expertise.

Then there was the matter of the notebook. Compton disappeared at odd times, only to reappear with that book. Fargo wanted a good look at it sometime. But first he might get more answers from the man who thought he had killed Compton.

The tracks vanished for dozens of yards at a time, but Fargo always got back on the trail. Crushed grass gave him his best trail signs. He was glad he had pushed on right away rather than waiting for the first light of day. The grass bent under heavy hooves would have popped back up, obscuring the trail, when sunlight shone on it.

Fargo rode eastward into the basin, the Laramie Mountains at his back. He found himself thinking of his last sight of Melissa and the way Compton comforted her. This thought almost spelled his death.

He was too busy worrying about what lay behind rather than what might be in front. Fargo's keen senses alerted him that something was amiss the instant before a bullet whined past his ear. He involuntarily jerked to the side and lost his balance, falling heavily to the ground. His Ovaro reared and pawed at the air, then snorted and dropped back to move between him and the gunman, as if protecting him.

Fargo was only slightly shaken by his fall. He rolled onto his side, drew his Colt, and began working his way through the waist-high grass. Many a time he had watched a small creature part the grass as it moved—and many a time he had gotten dinner by patiently waiting for the prey to break free of the concealing vegetation. He had to assume his sniper was at least that observant, and didn't plan on making that same mistake.

When he came across a deep ravine cut by runoff from a spring storm, he flopped belly down on it and began wiggling forward. To the sniper it appeared as if he had dropped back in the grass.

After slow counting, Fargo judged he had come far enough. He shot to his feet, six-shooter up, cocked and aimed.

"Damn," he muttered. He had misjudged how intent the sniper was on killing him and had assumed the bushwhacker would stick around to finish his victim. Fargo spotted another brass cartridge; this one was still hot from firing. He tucked it into his pocket and read the tracks in the ground. The heel mark with the large notch was prominent.

The assassin had fired, figured he had scored another kill, and ridden on. Fargo fumed at the man's callousness. It didn't matter to the sniper if he had seriously injured his target or killed him. The least he could have done was check his handiwork.

If he had, Fargo would have snared him quickly. Fargo jammed his six-gun back into his holster and put his fingers into his mouth to whistle for his horse. He hesitated, thinking the gunman might overhear. Then he decided he didn't care. Whether the man was alert or running for his life did not matter. Fargo was going to bring him in.

The Ovaro came to Fargo's whistle, and he jumped into the saddle. This time, as he rode, he paid more attention to what lay ahead. The gunman had shown his preference for ambush over face-to-face fighting, and Fargo didn't think he would change when he realized he had not been successful with his last killing.

At first light Fargo caught sight of a rider on the prairie. He considered taking a shot or two at him to get his attention, then decided to overtake him. Fargo rode faster, closing the gap between them and angling to trap the man along the Platte River. Getting across, even at the best fords, took enough time that Fargo was confident he could catch the man in midriver.

Less than ten minutes after the sun poked fully above the distant horizon, Fargo's quarry turned and spotted the trouble he was in. He frantically yanked out his rifle and triggered several rounds, but Fargo rode on stolidly. This spooked the man more than if Fargo had returned fire.

When gunfire didn't deter Fargo, the bushwhacker decided to make a run for it. He tried to get out onto the grasslands, but Fargo was close enough now that he could veer to the east and south and cut him off. This forced the rider back north, to the river.

Fargo had him bottled up in less than an hour.

"What you wantin' from me?" the man shouted. He had tried to cross the Platte, then saw how close Fargo was and what an easy target he would make in the raging water. "I ain't got no money. You go on now. Let me be!"

"Why'd you kill Paul Hancock?" Fargo asked, planning the best way to get the drop on the man. A few cottonwoods along the river provided scant sanctuary. The sparse vegetation also made it hard for Fargo to get closer without being ventilated. The sniper had shown his skill when he shot Paul from over a hundred yards.

"Dunno who that is," the man said. The words carried a bit of confusion, and Fargo guessed why.

"Why did you want to kill Justin Compton? You missed him and killed his guide."

"That who you said 'fore?"

Fargo knew the man was playing for time now. The sooner he was caught and hog-tied, the better Fargo would like it. He drew his Henry and took careful aim, waiting for the man to show himself. It required some patience, but Fargo was glad he waited.

The shot was almost too good to be true. The man swung around the thick hole of the cottonwood, rested his rifle against a low limb, and worked to sight in on Fargo. He was too late by seconds. Fargo squeezed back and felt the Henry kick hard.

His bullet was a little off target but not enough to matter. The slug ripped along the limb the man was using as a support, tore up his left hand, and wormed onto the side of the rifle receiver. The weapon flew from the man's injured hand and landed with a squish in the mud along the riverbank.

"You son of a bitch! You skinned my damn knuckles!" the man shouted.

"I'll skin you alive when I catch you if you don't give up now," Fargo shot back. He levered another round into the Henry's chamber and got off a second shot as the man tried to scoop up his fallen rifle and slither back to cover. Fargo's slug went wide but came close enough to force the man to give up trying to retrieve his rifle.

"I don't know you from Adam. You ain't got no feud, you and me. Tell you what. I'll forget how you shot me up and let you ride off."

"You're going to hang for murdering Hancock," Fargo said.

"I told you! I don't know no fella by that name."

"You were aiming at Compton, weren't you?" Fargo

looked around and saw a chance to gain the high ground. He shinnied up the trunk of a cottonwood and got onto the lower limb, affording him a downward shot at the man cowering behind another tree less than dozen yards off. From here it was an easy shot.

Fargo held back on making the killing shot. He wanted information as much as he wanted the pleasure of seeing the man convicted in a courtroom and then taken out and hanged for murder.

"What if I was? It ain't nuthin' to you."

Fargo had a good look at the man from his vantage point. The bushwhacker's flannel shirt was old, dirty, and ragged, showing years of hard use with little care being given for washing or mending. Heavy brown canvas pants like a forty-niner might wear had held up somewhat better to the wear and tear. He wore a floppy-brimmed black felt hat pulled down low on his forehead so his eyebrows were hidden and his eyes peered out barely an inch under the brim. He sported a stubble like sandpaper, interrupted only by a long pink scar on his left jaw. Jerky movements showed how nervous he was at being pinned down by Fargo's accurate gunfire.

Fargo took careful aim and squeezed back on the trigger. The Henry bucked and the target yelped in pain. The scruffy man grabbed at his leg and fell to the ground, howling in pain.

"You shot me, damn your eyes!"

"Don't move," Fargo warned. "I'm inclined to finish you off here and now for what you did to my friend." Fargo used the words to hold the man in place as he dropped from the limb and went toward him.

But Fargo had not counted on what might happen with a wounded rattler. The man flopped onto his side and aimed his six-shooter. A look of triumph blazed on his face as he fired.

Fargo reacted without thinking. He shot the man squarely in the center of the chest even as the bushwhacker's bullet tore through his right sleeve. A fragment of lead slug cut his flesh, but otherwise he was unharmed.

"You should have given up," Fargo said, staring at the dead man. A look of surprise was the last expression the killer would ever show.

Fargo wished it had turned out differently because he wanted answers as much as he wanted justice. A quick look at the man's heel showed the betraying notch. Fargo heaved a sigh of relief, knowing now he had shot the right man. He dropped to his knee and began rummaging around in the dead man's pockets, hunting for a clue as to why he had been gunning for Justin Compton.

He found a few scraps of paper that had been water-logged during a crossing of the Platte. What writing had been on them was long gone, only blue blurs of ink remaining. Less than ten dollars in silver rode in the man's shirt pocket. Nowhere did Fargo find anything to tell him why Paul Hancock had died.

Or why this man wanted Compton dead.

He stood and looked around for a good place to bury the body. It wasn't a chore he relished, but he wasn't the sort to leave anyone, even a back-shooting killer like this one, above ground for the coyotes to feed on. Fargo used a rock with an edge on it to scrape down into the muddy ground until he had dug a decent grave. He rolled the man into it, then covered him with the damp dirt until only a mound remained.

"I'd leave a marker if I knew what your name was," Fargo said.

"It was Les. Lester Wilkins," came the cold words.

Fargo turned to find himself staring down the barrel of a leveled six-gun in the hand of a man dressed all in black.

13

Fargo knew a gunfighter when he saw one. The man in black wore tight leather gloves, had his holster tied down with a rawhide string, and bore the look of a man used to killing rather than talking. His black clothing was dusty and a bit frayed but had been expensive not too long ago.

"I don't suppose you want to let me know your name so I can put it on a grave marker—one that you weren't even going to provide for poor Les."

"Your friend shot a man in the back. He didn't even have the nerve to come up close. He back-shot him from more than a hundred yards off in the dark."

A man standing just behind the black-dressed gunman laughed and said, "That sounds like damned good shootin' to me, Stack. Could'na been Les. Once I seen him empty a six-shooter inside a barn and miss the walls every time."

Fargo eyed the three men with the gunman. They were cut from the same cloth as the recently deceased Les Wilkins, lean and mean and uglier than sin. He didn't miss the threat of all of them with capable hands resting on the butts on their six-guns either.

"Do you go around shooting men in the back, too?" asked Fargo.

"I don't have to," Stack said. "Les got a hair up his ass and lit out on his own. What he did was on his own time."

"So you don't have a grudge against Paul Hancock?" Fargo saw the ripple of surprise pass through the tight knot of gunmen.

"Hancock?" asked the one to Stack's left.

"Shut up, Jesse," Stack said. "He's fishing. That's all."

"Why not make sure?" insisted Jesse. "You told him to wait for us. If Les upped and shot the wrong—"

"You didn't want Hancock dead, did you?" asked Fargo. "Who did you intend to murder?"

"Comp—" was as far as Jesse got before Fargo threw himself over Les's grave, hitting the ground and kicking up a spray of mud. He scrambled fast, got his feet under him, and dived behind the cottonwood as he yanked out his Colt.

"Shoot him," Stack said in his icy voice. Fargo realized he should have let them think Wilkins had succeeded in killing Compton. Now they would renew their hunt for their target and, with four of them trying, might accomplish what the one killer had not.

Bullets ripped past the tree trunk. Fargo heard several sink deeply into the wood, as if the four men intended to chop the tree down with their barrage. He chanced a quick look around and almost got his face blown off. Pulling back fast, he clutched his Colt as he waited for the killers to start dropping hammers on empty chambers. It didn't take long.

He heard a dull click and knew a six-shooter had come up empty. He waited for the second click before whirling around and firing. Jesse yelped like a stuck pig and grabbed for his bloody ear as Fargo's bullet took off a piece.

"He shot me!"

"Fools," growled Stack. The black-dressed gunfighter had not emptied his pistol the way his impetuous henchmen had. He fired three times, but Fargo wasn't presenting himself as a target any longer than necessary. He jumped back, then darted out to scoop up his Henry. This shifted the fight over to Fargo's favor. He had a mostly full fifteen-round magazine, and the killers were struggling to reload chamber by chamber since none of them carried loaded cylinders to replace their spent ones.

Fargo jacked a round into the Henry's chamber and

considered what to do. Poking around the tree, he fired at the men's standing horses some distance away. How he had missed them dismounting and walking over was a mystery, unless he had been too engrossed in putting Les Wilkins to rest and thinking too much about Compton—and Melissa.

"The horses! The son of a bitch is shootin' our horses now!" cried Jesse.

This caused enough confusion for Fargo to chance a dash to the cottonwood where he had first shot Wilkins. He got there, spun about, and dropped to his belly with the tree providing cover for him. Fargo began firing slowly, methodically, seeking targets that would kill rather than wound. He had to even the odds or end up in grave beside the outlaw he had already buried.

To his surprise, Stack rounded up his men and got them on horseback. For a heart-stopping moment, he thought the black-suited man would charge him, six-shooter blazing. The man then wheeled his horse around and galloped off, his three henchmen close behind. He let them go. Wilkins might shoot a man in the back, but Fargo never would.

Wiping sweat off his face, Fargo fetched his Ovaro and started back for Compton's camp. Throughout the day he doubled back on his trail, used weeds to hide his tracks, and tried every trick he could imagine to be certain he was not leading Stack and the others to the place where they could finish what their back-shooting comrade had started. He was not sure this was needed since Wilkins had already found Compton's camp, but the man had been cut off from the rest of the gang and had died before he could tell Stack what he had done. For some reason, Wilkins had decided to kill Compton on his own instead of fetching the rest of the gang.

For money? To show up Stack? Fargo would never know.

That Wilkins had tried to kill Justin Compton was the only thing that made any sense. Who in all Wyoming could hold a grudge against Paul Hancock? But this skirted the real question of who in Wyoming held so much rancor against Compton.

Fargo wanted answers and could only get them from Compton.

He reached the spot where the wagons had been parked at midnight, only to find the site deserted. Fargo dropped to one knee and saw that the expedition had started south, going deeper into the Laramie Mountains in the direction of the pass. He wondered if the rich man wanted to pan for more gold or if he hunted that mustang to break. Fargo doubted even Paul's death would deter Compton from pursuing his pleasure.

Then Fargo found the fresh grave with the inscription carved into a piece of broken axle.

PAUL HANCOCK
LOVING BROTHER
BRAVE FRONTIERSMAN

The work required to carve the words into the rounded, seasoned hardwood impressed Fargo. He wondered which of Compton's servants had done it.

He mounted and followed the tracks, noting that one wagon wheel wobbled. He guessed that Bruno had not mounted the straightest axle possible but had done what he could using green wood. Fixing an axle with materials at hand in this part of Wyoming was difficult at best. Fargo hoped that Bruno had found several likely prospects for axle replacement because the extreme wobble told him the wheel would break the new axle within a day or two of travel over such rocky terrain.

Fargo dozed in the saddle, letting his paint carry him through the foothills into the more rugged mountains. Whether through luck or skill, Compton had found the pass that would let his wagons make the trip over the mountains with the least trouble.

Fargo rode into the camp just before sunup the next day.

Justin Compton sat in the driver's box of the back wagon, his heavy hunting rifle across his lap. He said nothing as Fargo came even with him.

"Where are you heading?" Fargo asked.

"Away," Compton said, more somber than usual. "I couldn't bear remaining by Paul's grave. I thought it best to take Melissa away from there, also."

"I saw the grave marker. It was more than I expected."

"It took a while carving it," Compton said. He smiled ruefully. "I broke the blade of my best knife before I got halfway through. Next time, I won't be so verbose."

"You did it? Good work," Fargo said, surprised again. The lettering had been adroitly done by someone used to wielding a knife. "You should sell your carvings."

"I do not consider it a change of profession I am likely to make," Compton said, a small smile curling his lips. He quickly sobered. "What did you find? Did you catch his killer?"

"Yes," Fargo said, climbing onto the wagon wheel and into the box beside Compton. "Do you know a man named Wilkins? Lester Wilkins?" Fargo watched closely for any recognition. Compton shook his head.

"That's a new name for me," the man said.

"What about Stack?"

Fargo thought he had jabbed Compton with a knife. The man sat straighter and his finger tightened on the rifle trigger.

"Who is he?" Fargo asked more pointedly.

"I don't know anyone named Stack," Compton lied. He shifted on the hard wooden seat and lifted his rifle, as if he had someone in his sights. "I am growing tired of this part of the West. After breakfast, we shall all make haste to reach the other side of these hills."

Fargo would have hardly called the Laramie Mountains "hills." There were peaks tall enough to hold snow most of the year, but that wasn't what struck him most. Compton was not frightened—not exactly—but he wanted to hightail it away from Stack and his henchmen.

"These are pretty wide-open ranges, but there is law out here. We can find a federal marshal or a sheriff."

"Because of Hancock?" Compton shook his head vigorously. "That's water under the bridge. Nothing can be done to bring him back, and you said the man who had shot him paid the ultimate penalty for his crime."

"Wilkins worked for Stack, even if he had set out on his own," Fargo said.

"So Stack doesn't know where we are?" Compton's eagerness was almost pathetic.

"You don't have to tell me why Stack and his gang have it in their heads to kill you, but you owe it to Melissa not to risk her life. She and her brother are innocent of whatever's dogging your heels." Fargo paused a moment, then asked, "Why did you hire them? They obviously weren't competent guides."

A small smile crept onto Compton's lips, and he got a distant look in his eyes.

"They needed help but were too proud to take hand-outs. I knew they would be in the way, but it seemed an interesting experience to have them along."

Fargo didn't for one second buy Justin Compton as a philanthropist. More likely he had brought them along as toys to enjoy as much as his hunting and gold panning. Fargo went cold inside when he considered what sort of toy a man like Compton would consider Melissa. It might have been that she and her brother came as a set; if Compton wanted her to accompany him, he had to hire Paul, also.

"Is your trip about over?"

"We get to the other side of the mountains as quickly as possible, and from there it's an easy journey of a week to Cheyenne," Compton said, showing more knowledge of the terrain than Fargo had expected. Fargo wondered how much of the man's ignorance was feigned. Or how much Fargo had wrongly assumed.

"You know the pass?" asked Fargo.

"It's navigable if we aim for the middle of the Laramies," Compton said. "See those peaks? Smack between them. We'll have some steep hauling to get there, but it's not too difficult getting through, even with a crippled wagon." Fargo could not have picked the region to cross any better.

The sun poked up over the horizon, and Compton's servants began stirring, preparing breakfast. Compton left his post as sentry and jumped lightly to the ground when Melissa stirred. Fargo watched her as she moved about. She had never looked lovelier, even pale and drawn as she was. Somehow, the new day's sunlight gave a blush to her cheeks, and her blue eyes sparkled with a brightness that rivaled the cloudless sky stretching above Wyoming.

"Gather around, everyone," Compton called. "Mr. Fargo has returned with news of Paul Hancock's killer."

"Skye!" cried Melissa, seeing him for the first time. She put her hand to her lips as Compton sketched out what Fargo had told him about tracking down Les Wilkins and their gunfight. He left out any mention of Stack and the remaining gang.

"I feel obligated to terminate this doughty expedition. As a result, we shall make all haste through the pass and across the lower reaches of Wyoming until we reach Cheyenne. From there, we return forthwith to New York by the fastest means available. Now, Pierre has fixed another fine meal for us. Eat hearty!"

For all his bonhomie as he joked and talked with his servants, no one accepted this as a decent end to the expedition. The servants were as good at reading Compton's real mood as Fargo.

"Skye," Melissa said, coming up to him. "D-did you kill the man who shot Paul?"

"If you're asking if I shot him in the back, the answer's no. I tried to take him prisoner, but he wouldn't have any of it. We shot it out, and he lost."

"I didn't mean . . . Are you . . . Oh, Skye!" Melissa flowed into his arms and buried her face in his buckskins, quaking as emotion built to the breaking point inside her. She cried openly. "This is such an awful land. Why did Paul and I ever come out here?"

Fargo held her, even after he saw Compton's stern expression over such public behavior.

"You're going home now," Fargo finally said to comfort her.

"Without Paul," she said, sniffing. She pulled back and looked up at him. "Are you leaving now?"

"I'll see you to Cheyenne. From there it's not that hard a trip back East."

113

"I didn't mean—" She bit off her words when Compton barked orders to get into the wagons and roll.

Fargo knew what she had meant, and it wasn't in the cards. Even if he had been so inclined, he wouldn't fit into her world of polite society on the other side of the Mississippi River, and she certainly had no reason to stay on the frontier.

"You'd better get your gear into the wagon. Compton isn't going to waste time on stragglers."

This struck her as funny. Melissa laughed and then hugged him before gathering her gear and loading it into the supply wagon. She still struggled to get her skittish horse saddled but had gotten better at the chore. Fargo did not offer to lend a hand because he knew she would have taken offense at it. She needed to prove to herself that she didn't need help from anyone, be it her brother or Skye Fargo.

"Why don't you two scout our path?" Compton asked from the driver's seat of the lead wagon. The wheel swung wildly as it turned, threatening to come loose at any instant. "Please."

Fargo heard a bit of charity in the request, as if Compton wanted Melissa ahead of the wagons and safely away from anyone pursuing them. Anyone like Stack and his gang.

"All right," Melissa agreed quickly. "We'll find the best track over the pass." She put her heels to her horse's flanks and trotted off, her head held high and the wind catching her long black hair and turning it into banner of defiance against her heartache. Fargo followed more slowly, taking time to study their back trail. If Stack had made it this far, he was hiding well.

Fargo caught up with Melissa and rode along without saying anything for mile after mile. The dark-haired woman was lost in her own thoughts, and Fargo didn't want to disturb her. But the track they had been following grew rockier and more treacherous as steep hills presented themselves.

"Do you think the wagons can make it up this hill?" Melissa asked. "Or should we try to find a way around?"

"There's not much of a road, but this is it," Fargo said. "Others have made it, though I'm not sure if they were going this way or coming from the far side." The hill was steep enough to make him consider her suggestion of scouting another route. If necessary, they could use ropes and crude block and tackle to help pull the wagons up the slope, but from the way Compton almost ran from Stack it wasn't likely he would want to take the time to do the time-consuming rigging.

"You go around the hill. There might be some other way up that won't delay the wagons. I'll see how difficult it is getting up what you so optimistically call a road."

Fargo hesitated, not wanting to let Melissa out of his sight. Although Compton had not said as much, he had sent Melissa along to keep her safely away from Stack and his hired killers. Fargo looked back again and saw Compton in the wagons a mile back down the slope. Farther away stretched the foothills of the Laramie Mountains and a whole lot of emptiness.

"Go on. I'll see if there's an easier way to the west."

Fargo watched as Melissa painstakingly worked her horse up the steep, rock-strewn path to the top before he headed toward a likely spot off the trail that might afford a better climb for the wagons. It took him only a few minutes to realize there wasn't any hope of getting past on this side since a deep crevice opened up and ran deeper into the mountains.

He rode back and looked up to the top of the hill expecting to see a triumphant Melissa waving him on up. When he didn't see her, he gave the Ovaro its head and let the horse pick its way carefully uphill to the top.

"Melissa!" he shouted when he saw her horse—without the woman astride. Her horse whinnied and pawed at the ground, then backed away from the brink of the crevice Fargo had seen from lower on the mountainside. A mere glance at the rocky ground and the signs left told Fargo the story. Melissa had ridden too close to the verge, her horse had reared, and she had . . .

Fargo jumped from the saddle and ran to the edge, fearing what he might find.

"Melissa!" he called. She clung to a rocky ledge fifteen feet below. He had read the signs right. Her horse had thrown her over the edge of the cliff, and only pure luck had saved her from tumbling another hundred feet to the bottom of the crevice.

"Skye, be careful. The rock's so slippery," she called to him. But her fingers frantically sought a more secure purchase—and failed. Melissa slid a bit closer to the edge of the slope. She would plunge to her death at any instant.

"Hang on. I'll get my rope and—"

As he turned to grab the lariat hanging from his saddle, the rock under his feet crackled, shifted, and then gave way, sending him plunging after the woman.

14

Fargo kicked and struggled and grabbed for any hand-hold he could find. His groping fingers found only sharp rock that cut at his flesh and eventually betrayed him by coming loose. He tumbled over the lip of the crevice and began sliding toward his doom.

The same quirk of rock that had saved Melissa also saved him—for the moment. Fargo landed hard on the sloping rock ledge and threw his arms around a midsize rock in time to keep from tumbling over into the canyon. Melissa fought to keep on the slanting rock ledge only a few feet away.

"Hang on," he said.

"And you'll save me?" Melissa laughed in spite of her predicament. She sobered as the full impact of their double misfortune hit her. "Save yourself, Skye. I don't know how much longer I can keep from slipping."

As if her words were transformed into action, the rock beneath her legs broke off and went tumbling into space, crashing noisily against the sheer wall of the crevice below. Melissa gasped, grabbed frantically, and found a new spot that afforded a temporary refuge from death.

Fargo forced himself to look away from her and concentrate on his own dilemma. Melissa was right. He couldn't save her until he got himself into a better position. His feet dangled over the edge of the rocky ledge. His boots scrabbled until he found a toehold for his left foot. He pushed himself up gingerly and succeeded in lying on his belly along the angled ledge. Any sudden movement would cause him to slide off into the canyon far below, but for the moment all pressure was off his hands and feet.

He reached out, found he was scant inches from Melissa, then snaked his way forward until he could grab her wrist.

"Can you pull yourself up?" he asked. "I've got you!"

Fargo grunted and almost fell off the ledge as Melissa's bloodied fingers turned too slippery to hang on any longer. He supported her entire weight with one brawny hand around her slender wrist. She twisted slightly under him as she hung in thin air, the motion threatening to break his hold.

"Find a foothold," he gasped out. Her weight was agony on his shoulder because of their position. The muscles in his forearm began to knot and twitch, but to let go now meant Melissa's death.

"I can't—wait, there, yes!"

The slackening weight sent a wave of relief through his arm and shoulder that almost immediately turned back to pain. He feared he might have torn a muscle.

"I'll keep hold until you get back to the ledge," he said. "If you can find a better spot, go there. This one slopes too much." Fargo fought to keep from sliding off as Melissa worked around under him.

"I see it, Skye. I don't know if I can reach it. Wait, yes, I can. There."

"Melissa!" he cried. Her weight vanished as she pulled free of his grip. He looked down and saw only a hundred feet of empty air.

"I'll fetch you next, Mr. Fargo."

Fargo shook himself, thinking he was hearing voices. Then he craned his neck around and looked to the edge above him and saw Justin Compton pulling powerfully on a rope, Melissa dangling in a loop at the end. In seconds she vanished over the edge, safe and sound.

Fargo closed his eyes and tried to keep calm. He wanted to do something other than lie there, waiting to be rescued, but to have moved even an inch more would mean his own death. When the loop of rope smacked into his hand, he reached out, got his arm through it, and slowly worked the lasso over his shoulders.

"Pull away," he called. Then Fargo cried out as the rock ledge gave way under him. For a frightening moment, he tumbled and then snapped to a halt, the rope checking his fall. He swung into the cliff face and began hunting for toeholds and other grips so he could take some of the strain off Compton and work his own way up.

Fargo was no stranger to climbing rocks and found what there was to grip, but the handholds were precious few and far between. More than he would have liked, he had to rely on Compton's strength to pull him up to join a frantic Melissa.

He flopped onto the ground, getting his breath back. Then Fargo looked up at a grinning Justin Compton.

"Thanks," Fargo said. "You pulled my fat out of the fire."

"You were well on your way to pulling yourself out. I only speeded up matters," Compton said, dusting off his hands. "It was a good thing I reached the bottom of the hill and wondered what had become of you two."

Fargo sat cross-legged on the ground and saw where the edge of the canyon rim had broken free, first under Melissa and then under his own feet. Hindsight told him he should have been more careful, but at the time there had been nothing to hint at the danger facing him.

"Thank you, thank you both," Melissa said.

"This reminds me of the time I led an expedition up Kilimanjaro after the safari where I bagged two elephants and a lion. You can't imagine how hard it is bringing down an elephant." Compton looked at Fargo, then asked, "You do know what sort of beast that is, don't you?"

"I saw one in a traveling circus," Fargo said, not sure if he ought to be impressed with any of Compton's bragging. It was directed more toward Melissa, who ate it up.

"Then you know how accurate a shot it has to be to bring one of the monstrous beasts to its knees. As I was saying, when I climbed Kilimanjaro, I had to do it with nothing more than the tips of my fingers. Never saw a mountain so sheer or dangerous—even this one." Compton lifted his nose an inch, as if looking over the brink to the bottom of the canyon. Fargo noticed the man wisely did not get any closer. He had learned how dangerous it was here from his and Melissa's misfortune.

"So you've roamed all over Africa?" Fargo asked.

"Every square inch of the Dark Continent," Compton assured him. "I've seen black men—fully grown, too— who hardly came to my waist. But deadly fighters! They were fierce and used blowguns with poison-tipped darts. And then there were natives over seven feet tall. Giants!"

Melissa looked skeptical at this but said nothing as Compton rambled on with his tales of travel all over the world and the sights he had seen. At first Fargo thought he might be making up most of them, then wondered if they might be true. There was a ring of sincerity in much of what Compton said that gnawed at the edges of Fargo's disbelief, chasing it away.

"If you've been to all these exotic places, what are you doing in Wyoming?" Fargo asked. He whistled and got his paint trotting over from where it had gone to hunt for tough buffalo grass to crop.

"Why, this is as thrilling as any other place I've been. The buffalos, the natives on the warpath, the prairie fires, and . . . things," Compton finished lamely. Fargo knew the man had started to mention the danger and chance for immediate death, but that would have been like a knife in Melissa's heart, reminding her of Paul's murder.

Or was it the woman's feelings Compton protected? Fargo wanted to know more about the black-clad Stack and why he wanted Compton dead. In spite of all his derring-do, Compton was strangely silent on this score.

"We ought to see to getting the wagons up the hill," Fargo said. "If you lighten the load, the teams might be strong enough to pull all the way. Otherwise, we'll have to rig a rope-and-pulley system to drag up the wagons."

"That would take too long," Compton said briskly. A touch of irritation showed as he added, "We'll unload and leave behind whatever can't be brought up in the wagons."

"We can port up about everything, but it'll take time. We have the time, don't we?" prodded Fargo, looking for Compton's reaction. Everything the man did told of sand running out of an hourglass. He was running from Stack and wasn't going to discuss the matter with the hired help like Fargo—or even Melissa Hancock.

"Get to it, will you, Mr. Fargo?" asked Compton. "I believe Melissa needs to rest a spell."

Melissa nodded and hung on the man's arm. Fargo saw she was bewitched by his stories.

"Please, Mr. Compton, tell me more about Africa. I have read books about it, but I've never come across anyone who has *been* there. Are the jungles as dense and dangerous as the writers say?"

"More so, my dear, far more dangerous than anyone from this fair country can comprehend. More than the Pygmies and giants stalks those jungles. There are fierce animals no rifle can bring down. I once tracked a tiger . . ."

Fargo turned away, letting Compton continue to spin his stories of distant places and strange peoples. There was a more immediate job to be completed. He rode to the top of the primitive road up the hill and looked out over their back trail, hunting for any sign they were being followed. Fargo squinted, then shielded his eyes and wished he had a spyglass when he saw tiny pillars of dust in the distance. It might be nothing more than a whirling dust devil. Those miniature tornadoes were born and died within minutes.

This one lingered, leading Fargo to think it might be Stack and his gang of killers. Then again, others occasionally rode this route across the Laramie Mountains. This was the best, lowest pass in the range and drew travelers from a hundred miles away to funnel through. But most of the traffic came from the south going north. Who, other than possibly Guinard building his bridge at Fort Caspar, might be heading in the wrong direction?

"It's not Guinard," Fargo decided. If the French

trapper-turned-entrepreneur needed tools or food, he was likely to get his supplies along the Platte. Moving cargo, even against the strong current in the broad river, was cheaper and more could be packed onto a single barge than could be brought from Cheyenne in a dozen wagons.

He rode down the path to where Bruno studied the repaired axle on the lead wagon and Charles hastily went through the supplies in the second, tossing out what wasn't needed. The rest of the servants scurried about, not sure what they were supposed to do.

Fargo took charge, glad to see Bruno and Charles had already seen the obstacle ahead of them and had reached the only logical conclusion.

"Compton says to leave what you can't take up in a single trip. If there's something you need to keep, put it into a pile where the rest of the men can carry it up."

"My utensils!" moaned Pierre, tearing at his hair while Charles mercilessly tossed out box after box of rattling cooking gear. Fargo wondered what use any of it was when all you needed for a decent pot of beans was a big wooden spoon for stirring. He knew better than to point this out to the chef.

"I can take some up in my saddlebags," Fargo told Pierre. "Choose what you can't do without."

"He can do without all of it," grumbled Charles, showing that there was little love lost between the two.

Fargo motioned and a grateful Pierre began stuffing spoons, knives, and long-tined forks into a burlap bag. It rattled and spooked the Ovaro, but Fargo was more worried about the sharp points prodding the horse and injuring it. He settled the bag, made sure there was enough saddle blanket beneath to pad it, then rode to the lead wagon so he could grab the harness and keep the team moving. The last thing Bruno needed was a balky horse or one intent on rearing halfway up the steep slope.

"Slow and steady," Fargo called to the driver. He then tugged on the harness enough to give the horse the right idea. The wagon creaked and made sounds as if it might break down at any instant, but Fargo fought along with Bruno and the horses and eventually gained the summit.

Bruno nodded curtly, more than Fargo expected in way of thanks from the dour man. He snapped the reins and got the team pulling along the relatively level track leading deeper into the pass. Fargo took the chance to look back on their trail. The dust cloud had vanished, but he had the feeling that Stack and his men were narrowing the distance. He had done what he could to hide their trail, but there were only so many places on this side of the river, and Stack was certain to have found the wagon tracks eventually.

Fargo had simply hoped it would have taken him longer. He had no desire to shoot it out with the man and his henchmen. Heaving a sigh, Fargo cut loose the bag with Pierre's cooking utensils, letting it crash to the ground, then made his way back down the hill and repeated the trip up with Charles's wagon. It seemed to take an eternity, and Fargo spent half his time looking over his shoulder, waiting for Stack to overtake them.

At the top of the hill a final time, Fargo tried to spot the gang on their trail and couldn't. He wondered if he ought to hang back to stop Stack, then decided speed was a better ally than trying to shoot it out with the gunman and his cronies.

He trotted after the last wagon and soon overtook it. He rode past Bruno's wagon and along the faint trail until he found Compton and Melissa, riding side by side, lost in deep conversation.

"Ah, Mr. Fargo. I hear the rumble of wagon wheels. All is well, I trust."

"It is," Fargo said. He hesitated to mention the gang on their heels but decided he had no choice. "We'll have company pretty soon. Stack and his gang."

"Are you certain?" The sharpness in Compton's question showed Fargo he knew exactly who trailed them.

"Who's Stack?" asked Melissa, looking from one man to the other. "What is it you're not telling me? Skye? Justin?"

"Nothing, my dear, nothing at all. This reminds me of the time I was lost in the Sahara Desert outside Cairo. Fierce place, no water, no hope for succor. We . . ."

Fargo let the two ride on. Compton's tall tales were taking Melissa's mind off her woes—and he suspected they were also intended to divert attention from Stack and his single-minded stalking.

"Find a good place to camp," Fargo told Bruno. "Make sure it's somewhere you can fight off anybody attacking during the night."

"Sioux?" Bruno said, doubtfully. Fargo shook his head and said nothing more. He wasn't sure if Compton's servants knew of their master's predicament, but if they did, Fargo was sure they would never give him even one small shred of information. They were closemouthed and utterly loyal to their employer.

Fargo saw a rise to the side of the road where he might stand watch to be sure Stack didn't get past. The only problem would be the darkness. In the mountains, it got so dark he might miss a solitary rider and would have to depend primarily on hearing and even smell. Fargo found the way to the top of the hill steeper than anticipated and had to leave his Ovaro tethered at the bottom while he scaled it on foot.

Settling down, Henry rifle across his knees, Fargo watched the back trail until the sun sank and the inky darkness he had worried about held the land so tightly he could never hope to see even one of Compton's elephants coming along the trail. He gave up trying to make out figures in the deep shadows, retraced his path, and mounted his Ovaro. In less than an hour he reached Compton's campsite.

As he rode toward it, he saw how Bruno had banked the cooking fires. He was sure Pierre had complained bitterly, but the chef had to have something to grouse about or he wouldn't be happy.

"That you, Fargo?" came the challenge.

"Charles," acknowledged Fargo. He had seen where the man had wedged himself into a narrow crevice and wanted to tell him there were better places to stand guard, then changed his mind. If Stack and his gunslinger friends showed up, Charles might be safer there than in camp. He let the man slip back into his rocky shell as he rode past and entered the camp.

"Ah, Mr. Fargo, just in time to make certain we have no leftovers," greeted Compton. "Have a plate of Pierre's wonderful victuals."

"Thanks," Fargo said, taking it. He sank down and saw Melissa trying to make up her mind where to sit, beside him or next to Compton. She came over and sat beside Fargo as he ate.

"What's going on, Skye?" she asked. "Justin won't tell me why he is so edgy."

"Edgy? Is that what you call it? Never saw a man with more stories to tell, and I've come across a whole slew of yarn-spinners at the Green River Rendezvous. The mountain men save up their stories all winter long and will talk the ear off anyone who shows the slightest interest in what they're saying."

"You're doing the same as Justin," she said angrily. "Lots of words, no answer. What's wrong?"

"Nothing, as long as we keep moving along as fast as we did today," Fargo said truthfully. He wanted to get through the Laramie Mountains and rolling on level plains toward Cheyenne as quickly as possible. Justin Compton could head back to New York then and Melissa could move on to wherever suited her.

"That's not the complete truth," she said. "But it's all I'm likely to worm out of you, isn't it?"

"Don't make a mountain out of a molehill," he told her. "Why don't you get to sleep? We've got a hard day's travel ahead tomorrow until we reach the pass. Then it's all downhill."

"All right," she said. Melissa started to say something more, stopped, then turned and went to where she bunked down under Charles's wagon. Fargo made a circuit of the camp, saw that Charles was alert and on guard, and then unrolled his own bedroll. Compton spoke with his servants in low tones, pointing ahead and issuing orders.

With his six-shooter close at hand, Fargo went to sleep, only to come awake an hour before dawn. He grabbed his gun and sat up, not sure what was wrong. Pulling on his boots, he checked to see if Melissa was still asleep. She looked as if she had not moved a muscle from the time she had gone to sleep. Fargo knelt and touched her cheek. The dark-haired woman murmured, ran her fingers over his hand, and then rolled away from him.

Fargo counted heads and accounted for Bruno and the rest of the servants. Then he stopped beside Compton's bed stretched out on the far side of Bruno's wagon. The dark lump breathed slowly, regularly—and Fargo knew something was wrong.

"Wake up," he said, shaking the man's shoulder. Charles looked up at him and rubbed sleep from his eyes.

"What's wrong?"

"Why are you in Compton's bed?"

"He relieved me. It was a bit after midnight, and I was getting sleepy. Mr. Compton told me to curl up here."

Fargo hurried to where Charles had stood guard and found the crevice empty. Then he made a quick tour of the camp.

A cold lump formed in Fargo's belly when he saw that one horse was missing from the remuda: Justin Compton's.

15

Fargo spun, his hand going to the Colt holstered at his side, when he heard movement behind him. He relaxed when he saw Melissa.

"What's wrong, Skye? You're so jumpy."

He didn't want to worry her but saw no way around it.

"Compton's gone. I'm not sure why, or if he went on his own."

"You think he might have been kidnapped? By the men trailing us back at the Platte?" She came closer. Fargo looked around, not wanting to wake any of the others in the camp until he came to a decision that was best for everyone.

"I don't think he was kidnapped. There wasn't any fuss, and Compton went to Charles and made certain he wouldn't ask questions by relieving him of guard duty."

"Where did he go, then, if those men didn't take him prisoner?"

Fargo put his arm around Melissa's shoulders and guided her to the far side of the rude corral. The horses were becoming restless and would awaken those in camp. They stopped some distance off where they could talk.

"He's likely taking the bull by the horns and going after Stack and the rest of his gang."

"Go help him!" she said. "He can't take on men like that by himself."

"Like what?" Fargo asked. He had been careful to avoid discussing what he had seen and done after he tracked Les Wilkins to keep from upsetting Melissa more. "Has Compton told you about Stack?"

"Well, a little. I sort of caught him off guard, and

Justin said Stack was a terrible man, a gunfighter, who had been hired by someone who has it in for him. Justin wasn't too troubled. If anything, he seemed amused."

"Amused," Fargo said, shaking his head. "Wilkins shot your brother in the back because he mistook him for Compton."

"Poor Paul should never have put on that flashy jacket," Melissa said softly. "We buried him in it."

"Wilkins thought he had killed Compton and was riding back to tell Stack. These aren't men to be taken lightly."

"Then go help Justin!"

"It's not that easy. Compton left his servants—and you—here. Since he didn't ask me to go with him, that might mean he wants me to see you to safety in Cheyenne." Fargo's mind raced. Compton had skills he kept hidden. He was an accomplished marksman, there was no doubt he was adept at rock climbing, and he had used a knife several times with more dexterity than Fargo expected from the spoiled son of a rich man. Compton had left camp under no duress and with some plan in mind.

Fargo wished Compton had taken him into his confidence and let him know what was going on.

"We can take care of ourselves. Oh, you know I'm not the rugged frontier woman. Neither Paul nor I had ever seen a buffalo before we came to Wyoming, but you said the trip from here on isn't hard. Justin will be facing terrible danger if he tries to face down Stack. Help him, Skye. Please. For me, if not for Justin's sake."

She moved closer. Fargo took her into his arms. He had come to a decision already, and it matched what Melissa was asking. Bruno, Charles, and the other servants could get through the pass and onto the prairie on the other side of the Laramies on their own. From there—if they were careful—they wouldn't face any real danger. But Compton rode into a firestorm with open eyes, and Fargo was not certain the arrogant man understood the full peril involved.

"Skye, go after him."

"I will," Fargo said, looking down into the beautiful woman's fathomless blue eyes. He kissed her. "I will after a while."

"Good," she said. "I wouldn't want to send you into danger without some reward."

He kissed her again, their lips crushing passionately. Melissa's tongue sneaked between her lips and played across Fargo's until he opened his mouth just a little. Her tongue thrust boldly into his mouth then and dueled his with tongue. Their tongues touched and danced, retreated and plunged until they were both panting for breath.

"More," Fargo said.

"Gladly," Melissa answered. Her fingers stroked over his chest and worked lower to get rid of his gun belt. She then let him open her blouse so that her snowy white breasts spilled out. The faint light from the stars above cast those luscious silky mounds in liquid silver that Fargo had to touch, to stroke, to covet.

His fingers glided over the sleek cones until he came to the dark-capped tips. His fingers tightened on those buds until Melissa moaned and sobbed in joy. She thrust her chest forward to stuff even more of her breasts into his hands. Then she began moving in a sensuous motion, lifting and falling so she got the most stimulation possible from the way he held her.

Fargo concentrated on her delightful breasts and how he manhandled them, but he found it increasingly difficult to keep his mind on giving Melissa pleasure when her hand had curled around his manhood and moved up and down in a motion that sent lightning bolts throughout his belly.

He reluctantly slid his hands off her breasts and explored other parts of her lush body. Fargo liked the way the lust-hard nipples pressed into his chest after he shucked off his buckskins, but he liked the sleek flow of her naked flesh under his fingers even more. He stroked up and down her back and then found the twin globes, her buttocks. Cupping them, he squeezed and kneaded as if they were lumps of dough waiting to be baked.

"Oh, Skye, that's heavenly," she cooed. She kissed at

129

his nipples while she continued stroking along his rigid length. "Don't stop," she urged.

"Stop?" He had to laugh. "I'm just getting started." Then he showed her what he meant.

She cried out in surprise as he bent over, got his arms around her and completely upended her. This put Melissa's slender legs up in the air and caused her skirts to fall down, exposing her bare crotch. Her legs split apart in a delightful V, where Fargo buried his face. His tongue lashed out across her most intimate flesh and gave her the same kind of excitement she had been meting out to him.

Or so he thought. He held her firmly even after she wiggled and complained a little. He was too busy enjoying the dainty treat before him to pay much attention until he felt her wet lips and eager tongue working where her fingers had only seconds earlier.

Fargo's legs turned weak as Melissa's mouth worked erotic miracles on him, draining his endurance even as his need built like steam in a locomotive boiler. He sank to the ground, then carefully lowered her, their mouths still avidly lapping and licking one another until Fargo could not stand it any longer.

"Yes, Skye, I want the same thing. Now, do it now," cried Melissa. She got her skirts positioned under her rump and lifted herself off the hard ground enough so he could move into position between her wide-spread legs.

The tip of his manhood now sank fully into her molten center. Fargo gasped as he felt himself surrounded by tight, clinging, moist female flesh. For a second he could not move. The sheer delight of his position froze him. Then Melissa twitched her hips and began grinding her groin against his. This set off a reaction all the way down into his loins.

If he had been motionless before, now his hips flew like a shuttle. He wove back and forth, creating a tapestry of sheer desire in both of them. Every stroke was powerful, deep, and demanding. As he built speed, the friction of his passage into her molten core built until he could not deny himself any longer.

As he found release, he felt Melissa's entire body tense. She arched her back and cried out in passionate release. He continued a little longer, then sank down, both tired and invigorated by the lovemaking. Fargo stared at the beautiful woman and wondered if he was making the right decision.

She looked so soft and tender and helpless. Melissa smiled and reached out to touch his cheek with her long fingers. In the fading starlight she looked as if she had been cast in marble, in glowing silver, but no statue had ever been so vibrantly alive.

"Find him, Skye. I'll be fine."

"You were more than fine," he told her, catching her hand and kissing her fingers. Then she drew back and he knew what had to be done. Reluctantly, he stood, then helped her to her feet. It took them several minutes to get presentable again. By now some of the servants in camp would be stirring. The first light of a false dawn promised a new day, and it was time for everyone to do their chores.

Fargo kissed Melissa again, then left quickly. He didn't want to change his mind. He knew she would be all right since the real threat was Stack and his men—and Compton meeting them head-on.

Bruno and Charles argued over something, and Pierre was unloading his precious cooking utensils to fix breakfast as Fargo saddled his Ovaro and rode out. Compton's servants never asked where he headed or took much note that he was going.

Fargo would leave it to Melissa to keep order in the camp and get them all on the trail again after chuck. By the time the sun poked a sliver of blinding radiance above the horizon, Fargo was on the trail. Finding Compton's tracks was hard on the rocky terrain, but there was no question which direction the man was headed. While he might have run off, fleeing through the pass and leaving his party to their fate when Stack found them, Fargo doubted it. If even one of the stories Compton had spun about his hunting trips to Africa was true, he would never run from a fight.

Compton just didn't understand what kind of a fight he ran toward.

An hour after sunrise, Fargo found the hoofprints from Compton's horse pressed into a dirt patch along the side of the trail. He slipped from the saddle and bent down to examine them closely. From the sharp edges and the lack of erosion from the gently blowing morning wind, Fargo knew Compton could not be more than fifteen or twenty minutes ahead.

Checking his Colt and Henry to make sure both were loaded, Fargo continued along the path. He rode faster, knowing Compton probably had come upon Stack and his gang by now. But he heard nothing to warn him of a shoot-out in progress. In fact, he heard nothing to alert him to anyone else on the mountain trail.

Fargo glanced down at the ground now and then to be sure he still had Compton's tracks in view. Less than five minutes later, he stopped and frowned. Dismounting, he examined the ground more carefully, then back-tracked until he found a place where it looked as if Compton had ridden at a right angle to the path. He walked slowly, keeping the faint hoofprints in view until they, too, suddenly ended. Walking in a wide circle, Fargo hunted for the continuation of the tracks. He didn't find them.

He looked around, scratched his head and wondered how Compton had managed to vanish completely into thin air. From the way he read the tracks, the only direction the man could have gone was straight up.

16

Fargo grew more frustrated when he went back to the main track and still could not figure out how he had lost Compton. In time Fargo knew he could find the trail, but he had a sense that time was running out.

Fargo wanted to find the outlaws and have it out with them before Compton got too involved. Whether Fargo was doing this out of a sense of justice, because Stack and the others had been responsible for Wilkins killing Paul Hancock, or if he wanted to keep Justin Compton in one piece, he could not say exactly. It was just the right thing to do.

Riding to the top of a low hill, Fargo studied the trail Compton and his party had traversed the day before. A small grin came to his lips when he spotted a man dressed entirely in black making his way up the steep slope that had given the wagons with their tired horses so much trouble.

Stack.

All Fargo had to do was take Stack prisoner and the threat to Compton was gone. Somehow, Fargo could not imagine that all the men had an ax to grind with Compton. Stack was the linchpin. Remove him, and the pursuit was over.

As he turned to ride back to the trail where he could lay his ambush, Fargo froze. He stared down the barrels of two leveled six-guns.

"You shouldn't stick that nose of yours where it don't belong," Jesse said. "Now we got to blow it off."

"It's gonna be a pleasure. Les was my best friend," said the other gunman.

Fargo's mind raced as he sought some way out of this trap. He had fallen too easily to this pair of owlhoots. They read his expression and laughed at him.

"You wonder how we snuck up on you?" asked Jesse. "Simple as pie. We was already here, hidin' out over yonder." As he gestured with the six-shooter in his hand, Fargo sprang into action. He dived forward, using Jesse as a shield to keep the other outlaw from firing.

Fargo crashed into Jesse and they went down in a heap, rolling over and over on the stony ground.

"Shoot the son of a bitch! Get him off me!" shouted Jesse as he tried to get his pistol targeted on Fargo's gut. "I can't fight him much longer. He's too strong for me!"

Fargo kept rolling, his powerful hands crushing down hard on Jesse's wrists to keep the man from shooting him.

"I might hit you, Jess," the other man cried. "Stop foolin' 'round with 'im so I can plug 'im!"

"I'm tryin'," Jesse grated out. Fargo tightened his grip and forced the six-shooter away. He was gaining the upper hand but could not pin his opponent without getting shot by the man's partner. Instead, Fargo pushed downward with all his weight, driving Jesse's wrist into a rock until his grip weakened. The six-gun finally fell from numbed fingers.

Fargo duped the outlaw into thinking he was escaping when he momentarily let go. Jesse jerked around like a wildcat, but Fargo had suckered him. A brawny arm circled Jesse's throat and began choking the life from him.

"I can't shoot 'im, Jess," whined the other gunman. "He's blockin' my shot."

"Go on, shoot," Fargo urged. "Do it and kill your partner!" He cut off a little more wind when Jesse tried to speak. Fargo kept the pressure on until he felt the outlaw begin to sag.

Seeing that Jesse wasn't going to get away and not wanting to tangle with Fargo, the outlaw backed off.

"No, don't let him!" Jesse got out before Fargo choked even more of the breath from the man's lungs.

The outlaw turned and ran.

"Your partner's running like a scalded dog," Fargo said. "Where's he heading? You got a camp? Or is he going to fetch Stack?"

A gunshot rang out, startling Fargo. He stood up and hoisted the other man to his feet. He pushed Jesse ahead of him in the direction taken by the man's partner. Another shot echoed through the mountains. Then a small volley sounded, all from a six-gun. The last shot was deep-throated, vital—and undoubtedly deadly.

The silence wore on Fargo until he had to go investigate. He shoved Jesse facedown on the ground, then drew his Colt and aimed it at the man's back.

"Don't move a muscle," Fargo warned.

He looked up when he caught movement out of the corner of his eye. Fargo swung around, then relaxed a mite when he saw Justin Compton walking up, his heavy hunting rifle resting on his right shoulder like some soldier marching smartly on the parade ground.

"What have you caught there, Mr. Fargo? Why, it looks like a varmint. What do they call them in the mountains? Marmots? It looks too much like a weasel for my liking."

"What happened?" Fargo asked, shifting his attention back to Jesse. The outlaw had started to get to his feet but froze when he saw how fast he could die if Fargo pulled the trigger.

"The gentleman who decided to show a white feather was a remarkably poor shot. I gave him a fair chance, but he missed several times before I ended his foul life." Compton's words turned increasingly bitter. "What should we do with this one? I say, let him run."

"What? You'd let me go?" Jesse looked at Compton suspiciously.

"Did I say I was going to do that? No, you miserable cur! I said I'd let you run!" In a smooth movement, Compton brought the rifle off his shoulder and aimed it at Jesse. "I figure I can hit you anywhere up to five hundred yards with no effort at all."

"Compton," warned Fargo. He knew the man had cause to hate Jesse and his boss, but he wasn't going to let him shoot anyone in the back. "Don't do it. You're no murderer."

"You have no idea what I am, Fargo," snapped Compton. "Right now I am royally pissed. And when I get royally pissed, someone is sure to die!"

"Y-you can't let him murder me!"

"Compton, don't," Fargo said, not moving. He kept his grip around Jesse's throat to control the frightened man. "We can take him into Cheyenne."

"They'd just string him up for his part in killing Paul," Compton said. "I will save the court the bother of knotting a rope and finding a sturdy enough tree limb. Now get out of the way or I'll shoot both of you!"

Jesse gave a convulsive surge that knocked Fargo back.

"Compton, no!" Fargo shouted. But the man's rifle never barked death. It didn't have to. Jesse had run off, terrified of what Compton was about to do. He had gone too close to the edge of the hill where it dropped off sharply and tumbled over.

Fargo got to his feet and looked down the steep slope. Jesse had hit at least two large rocks hard enough to leave behind blood. A lot of blood.

"You want to go down and finish him off?" Fargo asked.

"Leave him for the buzzards," Compton said in an icy voice. He turned to Fargo and stared at him for a moment. "I thought you were tough as nails. You turned yellow at the thought of giving him what he deserved."

"I'm no murderer. Are you?"

"Not yet," Compton said. "But gents like him and Stack make it mighty easy to contemplate."

"Why does Stack want to kill you?"

"He has his reasons, and they're all monetary. He's a paid killer. I don't know him and he doesn't know me."

"Who hired him and his gang? Melissa didn't tell me."

"That's because I didn't tell Melissa," Compton shot back. "Look, Fargo, this isn't your fight. I hoped you would figure out I wanted you to see her and the others through the pass safely. Get back there and do it. I can handle these . . . these assassins."

For a moment words had failed Compton, showing Fargo how furious the man actually was. He had always been glib and easy with his fancy words.

"Why not take Stack prisoner and turn him over to the law? This might be the frontier, but no one likes a back-shooter or a hired killer."

"I have my reasons," Compton said.

"You don't want some lawman asking questions, do you? Does it have something to do with that book you're always writing in?" Fargo knew he had touched a nerve when Compton's hand flew to the front of his shirt and his fingers traced the outline of the notebook. That was more precious to him than even revenge against Stack for hunting him down.

"I do not wish to spend my time in court testifying when Stack might have friends on the jury."

Fargo knew a feeble excuse when he heard it but saw no point in pressing Compton. He had hit the target when he mentioned the notebook and wished he could get a look at it since this might explain everything.

"There are two of them left," Compton said. "I have to take care of this unfinished business."

"I'll come along," Fargo said.

"See that Melissa gets to Cheyenne," Compton said. Then he saw how determined Fargo was and shook his head. "This isn't your fight, Fargo."

"That's not right. Stack tried to kill me, him and his gang."

"There's not much of a gang left," Compton said. "Only one gunman and Stack." The words turned even more bitter. "Come along or not. That's your business, but keep away from me when I find Stack."

Fargo knew that hog-tying Compton and taking him back to his expedition would solve nothing. Stack was no more likely to give up his hunt than Compton was. This deadly affair had to end. Fargo hoped to keep it from becoming a bloodbath.

They rode back down the hill and onto the track leading north toward the prairie where the had entered the mountains. Fargo kept a sharp eye ahead but found his attention diverted often by Compton's odd behavior. The man would throw his head back and sniff furiously, as if he was hunting by scent like a wolf. Fargo started to remark on this when Compton spun in the saddle, his rifle coming up. He aimed his heavy hunting piece at a tumble of rocks a few yards away.

"Nobody's there," Fargo said.

"Stack stopped for a few minutes," Compton said.

Fargo rode to the rocks and made his way along a tiny game trail. His eyes widened a little when he saw the remains of a campfire. From the look of the ashes in the small firepit, it had been put out hours earlier. Fargo looked over his shoulder at Compton, wondering if the man had actually smelled the faint scent remaining after so much time or if he had picked up some other clue that Stack had been here.

"I've learned, Fargo," the man said. "You can hunt or be hunted. I prefer the former."

"Where do you think Stack went from here? We didn't pass him," Fargo said. He dropped to the ground and studied the traces left. Two men had boiled coffee, and then left.

"He's not retreating," Compton said. "Men like him have too high an opinion of their own abilities. He's still hunting me."

"Wait," Fargo said, when Compton started to retrace their route. "Stack and his henchman didn't go that way. They went up into the hills to the west."

"How do you know?"

Fargo pointed out a trail of spoor that proved he was right. He wondered what Stack was up to if he was after Compton. Heading in this direction wasn't going to get the gunman any closer to his quarry.

"I don't see it," Compton said. He walked around the abandoned campsite and shook his head.

"I'm right," Fargo insisted.

"Then let's go."

They rode through the rocky area and came out on a more level stretch within ten minutes.

"What's wrong, Mr. Fargo?" Compton was in a better

mood but still had a determination about him that showed he wasn't a giddy, spoiled rich man's son out on a lark.

"Why make it so hard to find the campsite and then leave a trail a blind man could follow?"

Compton frowned as Fargo pulled his Henry rifle from its saddle sheath. Then the man got the drift of Fargo's words and hefted his own rifle, looking around alertly.

"There!" both men shouted at the same time.

Fargo's shot was a fraction of a second before Compton's, but Fargo wasn't sure whose slug lifted the bushwhacker off his feet and threw him back over the rock where he had been hiding. Fargo levered another round into his rifle and put his heels to the Ovaro's flanks. This was no time to be lollygagging out in the open. They had taken out the last member of Stack's gang.

That left the leader.

Fargo hit the ground running, stumbled, and went belly down behind a rock as he studied the most likely spot for Stack to be lying in wait. He wasn't disappointed. He saw the black crown of Stack's hat rising from cover. His finger came back slowly on the trigger, but the report of another gun startled him.

Compton had fired too soon. His bullet ripped through Stack's hat, sending it flying through the air. If he hadn't been seized with buck fever, he could have gotten the head inside the hat as well. Or Fargo could have.

A flurry of shots ensued, Fargo firing to keep Stack pinned down. He hoped Compton had sense enough to circle and approach the gunman from the side. If they kept Stack bouncing from one direction to the other, they could wear him down and take him.

Fargo wanted him alive. Compton obviously intended for him to end up as buzzard bait.

"Hold your fire!" Fargo shouted to Compton. "You might have winged him."

"I don't think so," Compton shouted back. "Did you see him take a clean hit?"

Fargo hadn't. He gathered his feet under him, then sprinted forward, keeping low. Reaching a spot under where Stack had launched his abortive ambush, Fargo took a deep breath and then made his move. He rushed around the rock, ready to shoot at anything in motion.

"There's nobody here," Fargo called to Compton. He jerked his rifle upward when Compton popped up. "Can you see where he went?"

"He lit out to the west." The words were hardly out of Compton's mouth when they heard the pounding of a horse's hooves against the rocky ground.

Fargo clambered up beside Compton to get a better look. Compton lowered his rifle since he had no chance at a shot at this distance. But he had missed what Fargo's keen eyes spotted immediately.

Stack rode due west toward a dust cloud that would cross his path if he kept riding much longer.

"Sioux," Fargo said. "He's riding smack into a party of Sioux."

17

"Stack won't get away from them," Compton said, giving an accurate appraisal of the gunman's chances. "The Sioux cannot miss him if he keeps riding, but—"

"But what?" asked Fargo. "We have to warn him."

"He is a crafty killer. He knew I would find the deserted campsite and follow so I would blunder into his ambush. This might be a similar trick."

"How did you know Stack's camp was so close? I couldn't smell the ashes until I was almost upon it."

Compton smiled ruefully. "Stack knows me better than I thought. Hunting in Africa developed my sense of smell to an extreme level. Hearing means nothing in a jungle, where the vegetation drowns out all sound. The thick vines keep you from seeing more than few feet, but you learn how to distinguish one smell from another."

"He knew that?" Fargo wasn't sure he believed what Compton was telling him, but the fact was that Compton had found the remains of the campfire and he had not.

"He must have been given complete details," Compton's hand clenched the front handgrip of his rifle so hard his knuckles turned white with strain.

"Who hates you that much?"

"It doesn't matter at the moment. We are faced with a problem. Do we let Stack continue his wayward path so that he blunders into the Indian warriors or risk the chance that this is yet another trap he is setting for me?"

"He didn't have time to plan out any new mischief," Fargo said. They had not ridden into the ambush Stack and his partner had set—and that was the one supposed to eliminate Justin Compton once and for all. Why have a complicated backup plan when you were sure you had lured your quarry into a foolproof trap?

"You might be right, but however it is, I must go after him."

"The Sioux are ferocious fighters, and it looks as if they are on the warpath," Fargo said. "Judging from the size of this band, I'd say another twenty or more might be going north to join the village we spotted along the Belle Fourche River."

"Indeed," Compton said. He carefully loaded his hunting rifle and made sure the action worked properly. "Mr. Fargo, please go back to the wagons and see Melissa to safety. I can deal with Stack."

Fargo shook his head. Compton showed curious flashes of skill, but at no time did it seem he knew what he faced when it came to the Sioux. The Indians and their culture were a mystery to him. He might hunt elephants and buffalos successfully, but he would be the hunted one if he crossed the Sioux.

"Every minute we stand around jawing means Stack is another minute ahead of us," Fargo said. Compton did not look pleased at having Fargo along but said nothing as they trotted in pursuit of the fleeing bushwhacker.

They found a trail down the side of the rocky hill and soon lost sight of both Stack and the Sioux party out on the prairie. This worried Compton, and no amount of soothing on Fargo's part convinced him that they weren't going to surrender Stack to the Indians.

"He had another way down the mountainside," Compton said, seeing how slow their progress was. "He is a wily bastard. He must have figured out a retreat before setting up the ambush."

"Do you know anything about Stack, other than what you've figured out since he started after you?" asked Fargo. "Is he fast on the draw?"

"He has the look of a gunfighter," Compton said. Then he shook his head. "Stack killed my surveyor back in St. Louis before I started on the excursion, but I thought then I had taken care of him permanently by turning him over to the police. He obviously escaped the law and has proven more determined than I thought possible. I don't know anything about him other than Kohlmann hired him, and he only hires the best."

"Who's Kohlmann?" The name sounded familiar, but Fargo couldn't place it.

"There!" cried Compton, pointing. "Stack's riding for his life."

"Too late," Fargo said, seeing how a half dozen Indians broke from the main band and lit out after Stack. The black-clad man was an ebony dot racing along the prairie. And then that speck was surrounded by whooping, hollering Sioux. Their savage cries carried the few miles to Fargo and Compton.

"I lost sight of them," Compton said, standing in his stirrups. He sank down to his saddle, deep in thought. Then he said, "I've got to be sure he wasn't captured. He escaped before. I will not allow him to dog my steps forever, not after what happened to Paul."

Fargo agreed but for a different reason. In spite of all Stack had done and tried to do, he didn't deserve what he would get if the Sioux took him alive. They were painted for war—and the white man was their enemy. For a raiding party, or even a hunting party, to catch a lone rider meant hours of agonizing torment for their prisoner.

"How close can we get without being seen?" asked Compton. For the first time he asked Fargo for advice. Fargo took this to mean the man's natural arrogance was fading in the face of danger he was unable to cope with.

"If we stay behind them, they probably won't see it. This is a war party, and the braves will be pretty cocky, thinking they are invincible. Since they have a prisoner, they might pitch camp soon, though, so they can torture him."

"It's some time until sundown," Compton said, squinting at the sun dropping in the west. "How difficult would it be to sneak into their camp after sundown and see to Stack?"

"Damned hard," Fargo admitted, "but we don't have any choice. Neither does Stack."

143

They rode cautiously along the trail left by the Sioux warriors. Now and then Fargo saw small items the Indians had discarded that reinforced his notion that this was a war party. He saw a broken eagle feather, a beaded amulet, and even a bone handle from a knife along the trail. These were the types of items he expected from warriors, not hunters. What had riled the Sioux to make them rise up as a nation was less interesting to Fargo than avoiding all contact with them until they cooled down.

One on one or even a few at a time, he was a match for the Sioux. But with so many roving around Wyoming's prairies and mountains, he knew he faced not a single warrior but an entire tribe. Fighting them would be like tangling with a swarm of wasps. No matter how good he was at swatting them away, some would always get through to sting him.

The sting of a Sioux warrior meant death.

"Wait," Fargo cautioned, holding up his hand. They had ridden about a mile to the rear of the Sioux band, but something struck him as wrong now. Cocking his head to one side, he listened hard and came to the same conclusion as Compton, but for different reasons.

"They've stopped," Compton said. "I don't smell the dust in the air anymore, and there's an acrid scent—burning buffalo chips."

Fargo nodded agreement. He no longer heard the warriors' loud cries as they whipped each other into a fighting frenzy, nor did he hear their horses moving on the dry, drumlike prairie.

"We might have a good chance to rescue Stack before sundown," Fargo said.

Compton sniffed the air again. "Rain," the man said.

Fargo saw the way the clouds scudded low in the west, moving in their direction. The cloudy underbelly looked like lead, hinting at a downpour ahead. If the rain started soon, the Sioux wouldn't have as much time to practice their diabolical tortures on Stack. Even better, a heavy rain would shield Fargo from an alert sentry when he went after the Indians' captive.

"Not long, Mr. Fargo. I think we'll be drenched inside an hour."

"Then we ought to rest," Fargo said. "The next couple hours are going to be overflowing with trouble."

Compton laughed at this and said, "I hope the prairie isn't turned into a swamp. Getting away in knee-deep mud might be impossible, though I once stalked a hippo in a stream up to my waist. The mud at the bottom caught at my ankles and kept me from getting as close as I would have liked before it attacked."

Fargo tethered his Ovaro and rested in the shade afforded by the stallion as Compton rattled on about his hunting prowess. Whether he embroidered details or told the gospel truth wasn't for Fargo to say. All that mattered now was that Compton didn't jump the gun and bring all the Sioux down on their necks.

Fargo drifted to sleep, only to awaken in a start when a cold raindrop spattered against his face. He wiped it off and looked around. Compton had stood guard, his heavy rifle pointed in the direction of the Sioux camp.

"It's about time," Fargo said. "You stay here while I scout the camp."

"No," Compton said brusquely. "That will do. If you're seen, there will be hell to pay. We must go in quickly, decisively, with no hesitation or fear, and then get out of the same way. It's too risky making a second foray after Stack."

Fargo didn't want to go into the Sioux camp worrying about Compton making a misstep and said so.

"I have hunted lions and tigers. Tigers are the worst since they will turn the tables and hunt you. I know how to walk quietly, even in this terrain."

Fargo saw no way to keep the man away if he was bound and determined to join in rescuing Stack.

"The grass is dry now, but the mud will cause your boots to stick before we get to the encampment," Fargo warned.

"I am up to the challenge," Compton said, swinging his rifle around so the barrel rested in the crook of his left arm.

Fargo wished he would leave the heavy rifle with the horses but knew Compton had been right on one important point. Time mattered now. They had to get in fast and out even faster with Stack.

The rain began falling in thick curtains as they picked their way across the prairie toward the Sioux camp. Through the blowing rain Fargo occasionally saw sign of a fire, but all too soon even this guidepost vanished as the storm unleashed its full fury. He pulled down the brim of his hat to protect his eyes, but the rain blinded him on occasion. Glancing to his left to be sure Compton was still with him, Fargo pushed on.

The rain was bad, but the gusty winds proved worse. Fargo estimated they had covered less than half the distance to the Indians' camp when a sudden blast of wind almost knocked him off his feet.

"This is worse than a hurricane," Compton said, almost shouting in Fargo's ear. "A hurricane wind blows steadily. This on and off is disorienting me."

"That way," Fargo said, lifting his drenched buckskin-clad arm to point toward the Sioux. He had worried about their braves being alert while on guard duty, eager to find an enemy and lift a scalp. Now he feared they might walk over a guard and never notice.

The downpour increased until Fargo was virtually blind. If he had any sense, he would have gone to ground and waited for the worst to pass. But he dared not do that. If he could see better, so could the Sioux.

"Which way?" Compton had to shout to be heard over the whine of the powerful wind whipping across the prairie. The once-dry grass now tried to perk up as moisture seeped into the ground, only to be blown flat by the strong gusts.

Fargo thought he knew the right way, then realized he might have gotten turned around in the storm. He headed more or less in the right direction, but without seeing the camp he was only guessing. Dropping to his knees, he watched the way the rainwater puddled and ran down the rivulets cut in the once-dry land. Following the water as it flowed downhill would bring them to the Sioux camp.

Ten minutes later Fargo began to worry that he had made a mistake.

"There!" he said as a savage gust of wind blew a path through the rain, and he caught sight of the Indians' ponies staked out fifty feet to their right.

"We went too far west," Compton said, not pleased with Fargo's attempts to guide them through the torrential downpour.

"Circle on around," Fargo said, ignoring the man's implied criticism. He might as well have been blindfolded; they were lucky to have come this close. "The Sioux always tether their horses downwind from their camp so anything hunting them will get to the horses first and give them a chance to defend themselves."

"Even in a storm like this?"

Fargo didn't wait to see if Compton followed or stayed to complain. He rounded the crude corral holding the skittish horses and moved on to where the main camp would be. He stayed low to keep out of sight, letting the waist-high grass whip around him.

When he paused, Compton bumped into him.

"What's wrong?" asked the man. Fargo silenced him by pressing a finger to his lips. He pointed to a clump of grass ahead that swayed suspiciously.

Fargo advanced and saw a brave huddled under a fleecy buffalo hide, back to the wind and trying not to be miserable in the cold rain. This might be the camp sentry set to protect the horses, but Fargo didn't think so. He crept closer, drew his Arkansas toothpick, and then sprang like a cougar. His arm circled the Indian's throat like a steel bar. Fargo yanked back and exposed the warrior's throat. A quick slash ended the Sioux's life.

"Why'd you kill him?" asked Compton, coming up. "Are you taking his scalp?"

"No," Fargo said in disgust. "And be quiet. There are several more of them scattered around. He was doing a vigil as part of an initiation into a secret society."

"How can you tell?" Then Compton bit his lips and said, "Never mind. I bow to your superior knowledge."

Fargo moved on, hunting for the other young braves

who had been positioned alone around the camp to spend the night in utter silence, probably without food or water and wearing a hide from a buffalo they had slain with only a single arrow, as part of an initiation ceremony into the Buffalo Society. This confirmed Fargo's belief they were a war party out for scalps and blood. The last part of the initiation would require the braves to kill an enemy in battle.

Another lump appeared in the wet grass ahead. Fargo wiped rain from his eyes but did not move forward. To his surprise, Compton did. Before he could stop the man, Compton surged forward, rose to his full height and smashed the butt of his rifle downward. The recoil as the wood stock hit a rock, jolting him enough to make him stagger.

Fargo launched himself parallel to the ground when another nearby lump in the grass responded to Compton's attack on the mud-caked rock. The Trailsman caught the brave just above the knees and knocked him flat. The Sioux struggled and got free, his wet skin too slippery for Fargo to get a good grip.

The brave came to his feet, knife drawn. His lips pulled back in a feral snarl.

"I will kill you," the brave said in passable English.

"Kwa-nee-ta," Fargo said in Sioux. The startled brave hesitated a moment, giving Fargo the chance to crash into him again and bowl him over. This time Fargo ended up pinning the warrior's shoulders to the wet ground. A quick stab ended the man's life.

Panting, Fargo rolled off the dead body and wiped his knife blade clean in the grass.

"What happened?" asked Compton, crouched beside Fargo. "I thought you missed one and I—"

"You attacked a rock. The brave was a few feet away."

"What did you say to him?"

"I don't speak much in the Sioux tongue, but I told him to be quiet. Part of his initiation ordeal was to remain silent. When he realized he had violated his vow, I hit him—hard."

"How many more are out there?"

"Not many, unless I miss my guess," Fargo said. Seldom did the Sioux initiate more than a half dozen of their most valiant warriors into the secret society. In a band this large, there might be one or two more, but Fargo wasn't inclined to look for them. They would have been spaced far enough apart to isolate them from the rest of the camp. Killing two opened a broad route in and out of the camp.

Fargo kept low and moved toward the main camp without finding any other initiates in the tall grass. The rain was slackening a little, allowing him to get his bearings. He tugged at Compton's sleeve and pointed to a spot a few yards away. Two braves sat in front of a small fire, trying to keep it going in the downpour. Beyond them, partially hidden by the grass, lay another man.

"Stack," Compton said.

Fargo nodded. No Sioux wore boots like those poking out—not yet.

"Stay here," Fargo said. "Wait! Don't argue. Keep the two braves in your sights. If I can't get Stack free without alerting them, you'll have to shoot them, then take off like the demons of hell are on your heels."

"They will be, won't they?" asked Compton, a crooked grin on his lips.

"Worse than anything you've ever seen in Africa," Fargo agreed. "But the rain will work in your favor, so you might be able to get back to the horses ahead of them. Get out of here. Don't wait for me—for us."

"I have to know if Stack's alive," Compton said.

Fargo wasn't going to argue. Either Compton would do as he had been told or they would both end up staked out alongside Stack to die. Moving like a ghost through the rain, Fargo came to the spot where Stack lay. Not five feet away the two Sioux huddled around their fitful fire, struggling to eke out what warmth they could.

Fargo got close enough to see that Stack was still alive. The man's eyes went wide, and he started to call out. Fargo clamped his hand over the man's mouth, then looked up to see if the two guards had been alerted.

He heaved a sigh of relief when he saw the two braves

ignoring Stack, trying to get even more heat out of their buffalo-chip fire. Looking down at the smoldering fire kept them from watching their prisoner.

With a determined yank, Fargo pulled one stake out of the rain-softened ground. Without the downpour, that stake would have been almost permanently hammered into the hard ground. Fargo quickly pulled another out and freed Stack's other hand. By leaving the stakes behind and evidence that the man and escaped on his own, rather than leaving severed rawhide bonds, Fargo hoped to win a few extra minutes after the guards discovered their prisoner missing.

"Why are you doing this?" asked Stack.

"Shut up and go where I tell you." Fargo shoved the man deeper into the grass, began laying a false trail, then had Stack go in the opposite direction. Repeatedly, Fargo did what he could to keep their tracks to a minimum and confuse any Sioux coming after them.

Fargo reached the point where he began worrying he was spending too much time with his diversions and not enough on simply escaping. He knew the Sioux would find them if they were determined enough—and they would be, especially after they found two of their finest braves with slit throats.

He shoved Stack forward, in the direction of their horses. He considered stealing a pony for the bushwhacker to ride but decided it was too risky. The horses would rear or whinny and draw unwanted attention from the camp. A few braves Fargo could fight, but not twenty or more.

Stack kept trying to protest, to complain, and Fargo kept him quiet and moving as fast as possible through the tall grass.

"Our horses are a half mile that way," Fargo said, finding the spot where he had killed the first Sioux. "Walk fast, don't look back, and—"

Stack stopped, then went flying. He crashed to the ground and lay still. A Sioux warrior had smashed the butt of a rifle into the side of his head.

Fargo went for his Colt but froze when he saw the

Indian lower the rifle and point it straight at him. He was fast, but there was no way he could outstrip a bullet.

A feral grin crossed the Sioux's lips, and then the loud report of a rifle stunned Fargo.

18

Fargo took a step back at the sharp crack of the rifle. The Sioux brave's grin faded slowly and his rifle dropped from his dead fingers before he toppled like a tree in the forest. The warrior lay facedown on the ground as a small cloud of gun smoke drifted over his corpse. Then the rain and wind whipped away the heavy odor.

"Thanks," Fargo said, not needing to turn to see that Compton was in the grass to his right.

"I wouldn't want anything to happen to you," Compton said, levering another round into his rifle. He poked the dead brave and got no response. "I got him directly in the heart. He died instantly."

"Damned fine shooting," Stack said. He had quickly come to. Rain ran down his face. The outlaw wiped it off, then turned pale when he saw Compton turn and aim his heavy rifle directly at him.

"It's time to finish the hunt," Compton said, his finger drawing back on his trigger.

"Wait!" cried Fargo. "You can't gun him down in cold blood."

"It's not in cold blood," Compton said, his lips pulling back in a feral snarl. "It's in hot blood. He killed my surveyor, sent out the back-shooter who murdered Paul, and then tried to shoot me in the back!"

"Hold on," Fargo said. "We're in the middle of a Sioux war party. They must have heard the rifle shot. They're going to find their prisoner's gone and be after us in a flash."

"Then I need to dispose of this piece of trash so we can ride on unencumbered," Compton said, his anger hardly in check. Fargo saw how dead serious he was about killing Stack. The black-dressed gunman held up his hands and shook his head, then dropped to his knees as he pleaded for his life.

"Compton, don't lower yourself to his level."

"If I kill him my troubles are over. I save the law the cost of a trial and formal execution. He'd swing, unless Kohlmann bought the judge and jury. That's something I don't want to happen because Stack would come after me again. This is as much punishment for his part in killing Paul Hancock as it is trying to murder me. A paid killer. Ha!"

"You're better than that, Compton," Fargo said, stepping up. Stack tried to slip away, but Fargo grabbed the man's collar and threw him flat onto the muddy ground at his feet. "Do you want this man's blood on your hands?"

"I'm a hunter. Killing is not that foreign to me, Fargo."

"A man isn't a buffalo or an elephant."

"I agree. This one is less than dirt to me. I have great respect for those noble animals."

Fargo's hand flashed to his Colt. He drew, cocked, and fired in a smooth motion. A half dozen yards away a Sioux brave jerked at the impact of the bullet in his chest and staggered. Compton turned and fired and removed the threat permanently.

"Very well," Compton said, lowering the smoking muzzle of his rifle. "We ought to discuss this matter somewhere away from here."

"Thank you," gasped out Stack.

"Shut up," Fargo said, grabbing the man's collar and pulling him to his feet. "You're going to have to run like your life depends on it. And it does."

Fargo pushed him ahead as they made their way through the wet grass to where they had tethered their horses. His Ovaro tried to pull free when it saw its master. Fargo patted the horse's neck, then mounted. He silently pointed in the direction he wanted Stack to run. The gunman took off at a dead run that Fargo knew he could never maintain. Slower but at a pace he could maintain all day long, Fargo put the Ovaro into a trot. He glanced to his left and saw Justin Compton glowering as he rode.

The rainstorm turned heavier as they rode. For this Fargo thanked his lucky stars. Any trail they left would be wiped out as the rain drained off and carried surface soil down into washes and perked up dry stalks of grass they might have crushed. The Sioux were good hunters, but it would require a miracle for them to find the men who had sneaked into their camp and rescued a prisoner from under their noses.

· "P-please, I can't go much more," panted Stack.

"Do you want to tell Compton that? He's itching to leave you right here for the coyotes."

"No, no," gasped Stack. The man picked up the pace again. By the time they reached safety, he would be entirely tuckered out and unlikely to escape.

The rain began to let up; then the wind cleared away the clouds to leave the bright blue Wyoming sky stretching from horizon to horizon. The wind made it chilly as it blew across the damp prairie, but the chill turned to outright cold by the time they reached the foothills leading back into the Laramie Mountains.

Fargo saw that Stack was at the end of his rope and signaled Compton to take a rest. It was time to have it out with the man over gunning down Stack.

"This looks like a good place to die," Compton said. He swung his rifle around, but Fargo grabbed the barrel and held it off Stack, who could do little more than stand with his hands on trembling knees, panting and wheezing.

"Who's Kohlmann?" Fargo asked. "He's the one you have the real quarrel with. Stack is nothing more than a hired hand."

"A hand with his finger curled around a trigger," Compton said. Fargo wasn't able to argue that point and didn't try.

"Convince me murdering him is the right thing to do," Fargo said. He heard Stack flop to the ground and start to protest. A cold glare in the outlaw's direction silenced him.

The change of tactics caused Compton to recoil and stare at Fargo in wonder.

"There's nothing I can say that will convince you of that," Compton said, realizing where Fargo's sentiments lay. "Aubrey Dawks was my surveyor for a half dozen years and I counted him as my friend. Stack gunned him down as Aubrey and I left a private club in St. Louis. I made a mistake then, tracking down Stack and turning him over to the police. It was a mistake because he is here, possibly escaped but more likely out of jail because Kohlmann bribed the police captain."

"Why are you in Wyoming?"

"You get right to the core of the matter," Compton said. He spoke slowly, carefully, but his eyes never left Stack. "I'm not out West on a lark, on a hunting trip. I enjoy hunting, true, but it is only a convenient story to tell, should anyone wonder. My father is president of the Atlantic Central Railroad, and I'm chief construction engineer."

This drove home to Fargo how little he really knew of Justin Compton.

"That surprises you, Mr. Fargo? Good. I try hard to appear the ne'er-do-well. It's also true I enjoy hunting and am quite good at it."

"All that about African safaris was true?"

"What I told you, yes. What I failed to mention was going to Africa to learn railroad construction techniques over a variety of terrains. I learned how to put down ten miles of track a day across a prairie like Thunder Basin by studying the British system used to cross the veldt. And a mile a day or more is possible through mountains, even the Laramies, using German building methods."

"Kohlmann?" asked Fargo.

"He is a German railroad magnate and has laid track all over Europe and Africa. I learned from him, but I was incautious telling him my reasons for studying his construction system. I had not known at the time that he is a silent partner in the Ohio Southern, making him a potential competitor."

"Why are you out here? In Wyoming?" Fargo got a

cold lump in the pit of his belly because he thought he knew the answer and did not like it.

"There will be a transcontinental railroad built one day soon, Mr. Fargo. I intend the Atlantic Central to reap the benefit of linking one coast with the other."

"The notebook," Fargo said. "You've been making notes about the best route."

"This part of the country is flat but difficult to build across because of the lack of trees to cut for railroad ties. But if we supply along track already laid, we can bring ties from across the Mississippi, if necessary. There are other considerations. Rights of way, the type of soil and how it might settle . . ."

Fargo stopped listening as Compton rattled on in all the other details that he had recorded faithfully in his notes. He realized that, at last, he was getting the full story from the man, and it bothered him greatly. A railroad across Wyoming meant settlers coming in, plowing up the prairie where the buffalo herds now cropped the grass and turned the world to thunder with their mighty stampedes. More than this, people would pass through on their way to other, even more remote areas, areas Fargo considered home.

"Kohlmann is a ruthless son of a bitch," Compton went on. "He will stop at nothing, including killing me."

"Is that true, Stack?" Fargo asked. He prodded the gasping man with the toe of his boot.

"Don't know about him, 'cept his money's good."

"What's a man's life worth?" Compton started to lift his rifle again, but Fargo held it firmly. The expression on Compton's face told Fargo more than before. He wasn't as angry at Stack—and Kohlmann—for trying to kill him as he was that Paul Hancock had died. Since Compton had never held Paul in that high an esteem, Fargo put all the pieces together and realized Compton really was sweet on Melissa.

That explained a great deal of the Hancocks' peculiar employment. Compton was experienced from his expeditions throughout Africa and knew they were greenhorns. He had not cared, as long as Melissa came along. Compton was angry with Stack for killing his surveyor but was even angrier because the gunman was accountable for the death of the brother of the woman he loved.

"I'll take him in," Fargo said. He inclined his head to one side to get Compton out of Stack's earshot. The two rode a ways off, but both kept a sharp eye on their captive.

"What are you saying?" Compton demanded.

"Melissa wouldn't want anything to do with a man capable of killing in cold blood, even if that man was responsible for her brother's death." Fargo saw this shot hit the mark.

"She wouldn't, would she?" mused Compton. "What are you suggesting? I won't let you set him free. He's got to pay for what he's done. He and Kohlmann both!"

"I agree," Fargo said. "There's nothing I can do about this Kohlmann. You'll have to deal with him yourself once you're back East."

"What are you going to do with Stack?"

"I'll keep him safe and sound for a week or so, let you and the rest of your party get to Cheyenne. You might warn the federal marshal there that I'm on my way with a prisoner. By the time I turn Stack over to the law, you can be well on your way home."

"Why not accompany us to Cheyenne?" asked Compton.

Fargo pursed his lips, thought a moment, then said, "This makes it easier on Melissa. She never has to set eyes on Stack. I wouldn't want her traveling with the fear that the man who caused her brother's death was so close."

There was another reason, too, one that Compton saw right away. If Fargo hung back, Compton had less competition for Melissa's affections. What she and Fargo had was something she would remember for quite a spell. But she didn't belong in Wyoming or anywhere without servants or a sturdy roof over her head. She was city-born and bred and fit better in Compton's world than she ever could out West.

Maybe she would be back when Compton's railroad

cut across the Wyoming prairie on its way to the Pacific. Fargo doubted he would be around to see her if she did return because he wanted to be as far from that railroad as he could get.

"Let's get back to the expedition. You can come along that far," Compton said. Fargo nodded.

They got a dog-tired Stack walking again. The trip up the steep slopes into the Laramie Mountains kept their captive scrambling and tuckered him out so much that he was no trouble at all when they pitched camp that night. Even if he had tried to sneak off, Fargo knew Stack could never get far enough to escape.

Before dawn they were on the trail again and reached a hill looking down into the pass across the mountains just as daybreak lit the camp. Fargo let Stack take a rest as he watched the bustle in camp. The faint cooking odors from one of Pierre's fabulous meals drifted up to him and made his mouth water. Bruno and Charles worked to properly repair the front axle on the damaged wagon now that they had access to sturdy wood—and Melissa Hancock stood, stretched, arms high over her head and then went to work getting the equipment ready for the day's journey.

The sunlight caught her dark hair and triggered Fargo's memories of its smell, its texture, the way it flowed when the wind blew. He would miss her, but she was better off with Justin Compton. The railroad engineer could provide her all the things she had lost in life, except for her brother. That emptiness would remain. Fargo hoped Compton could fill it, at least partially.

"Time to part company, Mr. Fargo." Compton thrust out his hand. They shook.

"It's been quite a journey," Fargo said.

"That it has, sir, that it has." Compton grinned when he spotted Melissa. "Things are looking up for the rest of the way home."

"Don't worry about Stack. I'll see that he stands trial for what he's done. Chances are good he's got more than one wanted poster out on him, too."

"I'll be sure that the marshal understands how important it is to me and how he should check with the authorities in St. Louis concerning poor Aubrey's death," Compton said. "And I will leave five hundred dollars in an account under your name at the bank."

Fargo had forgotten that he had been working for Compton and had not been paid yet. This was more than he expected.

"Have a safe trip back to New York," Fargo said.

Justin Compton tapped his fingertips against the brim of his hat, grinned at Fargo, then put his spurs to his horse's flanks as he galloped through the pass toward his camp and Melissa Hancock.

Fargo wondered what Compton would tell the woman, then decided it did not matter. Melissa would accept whatever he said and be happy with Compton.

"You look plumb beat," Fargo said to his prisoner. "Why don't we take a break? For an hour."

As Stack rested, Fargo watched Compton and Melissa ride off at the head of their small wagon train, side by side. Long after they were gone he stared at the barren mountain pass; then he mounted and started Stack on the trail to Cheyenne and the justice he so richly deserved.

LOOKING FORWARD!
The following is the opening
section from the next novel in the exciting
Trailsman series from Signet:

**THE TRAILSMAN #243
WEST TEXAS UPRISING**

*West Texas, 1859—A man's good name
is his worth, insured by a steady hand
and hot lead.*

"Excuse me. Is this seat taken?"

A tall man in buckskin looked up from his study of the menu in the dining car of the El Paso Flyer.

The constant back-and-forth swaying motion of the passenger train caused the woman who had asked the question to place a slim hand on the edge of his table to steady herself.

She was in her early twenties, attired for travel in pressed crinoline. Wisps of blond hair curled from beneath a stylish bonnet that matched her dress. Her eyes were blue and radiant with intelligence. Her prominent chin was slightly cleft, making her all the more attractive, in Fargo's opinion. She had a curvaceous figure, which the severity of her clothes could not conceal. Her breasts were upthrust, her hips round and firm. She held herself with a proud, almost aristocratic bearing, he noted, and yet she exuded a sunny, friendly-to-the-world openness.

A glance around told Fargo that the seat across the table from him was the only vacant one in the dining car.

The atmosphere in the dining car was comfortable and busy, abuzz with table chatter, the clink of silverware and dishes, and the comings and goings of efficient waiters. The Texas prairie, rolling by outside the train-car windows, barren except for scrub brush and rock formations in the distance, was acquiring a golden patina as the sun descended lower in the western sky.

Fargo half rose, gesturing. "Please, ma'am. Have a seat. I'd appreciate the company."

Fargo had done all right financially by his last job, and he saw no reason not to return to El Paso in comfort. His horse—the beloved Ovaro stallion that was his one true friend—awaited him in El Paso, and he had enough folding money to take his time picking and choosing where his next dollars would come from. He was returning from having freelanced a job for the Rangers, who were undermanned in these parts. Fargo had signed on to escort a prisoner to Austin so the prisoner, a convicted murderer, could testify in an important trial. Fargo had earned his pay, which was another reason he didn't feel guilty about splurging on his return trip to El Paso.

And here he was, aboard a train due in El Paso at dawn, making the acquaintance of this charming young woman. He was glad he'd freshened up in his Pullman car compartment before coming to dinner.

She was sizing him up exactly as he had her, assessing him and appearing satisfied with what she saw.

"Thank you. You're very kind." She seated herself primly across from him as he settled back down. She extended a hand. "Lara Newton, of Boston, Massachusetts."

Her handshake conveyed confidence tempered with femininity, which he found arousing. A tingling sensation passed from her palm to his and went through him, warming his loins. He tried to keep this from showing in his expression.

"Skye Fargo, from down the road a piece."

"Down the road a piece?" She arched an eyebrow good-naturedly. "That's rather vague, isn't it?"

"With all due respect, ma'am, out here it isn't polite to ask questions about a person's background."

"I see." She regarded him with mild amusement. "Well then, the hell with being polite."

Fargo blinked. "Beg pardon, ma'am?"

"I said, the hell with being polite. I happen to be used to living my life flying in the face of social norms, Mr. Fargo. That's the way things were—I should say, are—with the family in Boston. And if I breach social etiquette in this quaint backwater of our great nation"—she nodded to the prairie speeding by outside the window—"then so be it. Frankly, I don't give a damn."

Fargo grinned. It made him look like a friendly bear. He had always liked spirited wenches.

"You're a plainspoken one, miss. Well, let's see now. This train's heading west, and my horse is waiting for me in El Paso. So you go ahead and decide where I'm from, if you've a mind to. But you might want to cut down on being so dang forward."

"I shouldn't act as I wish, you mean?"

"I'm just saying."

"I'm a woman on a mission," she said, "and I've got money back home that can buy me out of any trouble I get into."

"There's one kind of trouble they won't be able to buy you out of."

"And what's that?"

"Catching a bullet between those pretty eyes of yours," said Fargo. "That would be hard to buy your way out of, wouldn't it? The exit wound would turn the back of your head into one hell of a sticky situation."

She winced. "Are you threatening me?"

"Threatening you? Heck, ma'am, I barely know you, and I'm starting to sort of hope it stays that way."

"Well."

He sighed. The tingling sensation within him had subsided, but not his appreciation of her beauty. The warmth in his loins hadn't subsided either.

"Ma'am, I reckon if we're going to be traveling companions for the course of this meal, we may have to work at understanding what each other is saying."

She nodded in agreement. "I reckon," she said dryly.

A waiter appeared with a menu for her. She glanced it over as Fargo gave the waiter his order for a steak-and-potato dinner.

The woman across from him surprised Fargo when she handed the waiter the menu and said, "I'll have the same."

The waiter paused in writing on his paper pad. "Begging your pardon, ma'am, but that's a mighty lot of food for a female, if you don't mind my saying so. Might I recommend the filet mignon?"

"I'm hungry," she said. Her eyes were locked to Fargo's when she added, "I have a big appetite."

"Yes, ma'am." The waiter departed.

Lara Newton smiled a pretty, engaging smile. "I really should apologize, Mr. Fargo. I must seem awfully uppity to you."

"You've got your share of salt," Fargo conceded.

"May we begin again? It's been a long journey for me. I'm afraid my nerves are frayed. I didn't mean to be cross. Will you forgive me?"

Now this is more like it, thought Fargo.

"No harm done," he said.

"The fact of the matter is, although I sometimes choose to behave like a shrew, I have grasped the rudiments of Western etiquette since about, oh, I suppose, Kansas City." Her expression grew serious. "I really wasn't trying to be impolite. The fact of the matter is, I'm looking for a man."

"You're looking for a man to do what?" he asked, hopefully.

"I'm looking for a man to help me find my brother. I need to know something about the man I hire. That's reasonable, isn't it?"

"Preferable, I'd say, from your perspective. And you want to hire me?"

"I believe I do, yes. I can offer you a substantial retainer."

"Yeah. You said Boston."

"My family is quite wealthy, as a matter of fact. They're aware of what I'm doing, I should say, although Father particularly disapproves of my undertaking."

"Finding your brother?"

"Yes. I've been on the lookout for the right man to help me since I first left Boston—a man who is resourceful, tough, hardened by experience and this environment." She nodded again to the darkening prairie beyond their dining car window. "A true man of the West."

"I can't be the first able-bodied fellow you've encountered."

"Most of the men in the East, even the tough ones, wouldn't last a week out here," she said. "Some of the men I've considered along the way showed grit, but too often displayed a slowness of mind or a brutish side when I engaged them in conversation."

"The way you did with me?"

She nodded. "As I did with you."

"I reckon I'm flattered, although I've got to say that I believe you're moving this conversation along a mite fast."

"Nimble is the word you're looking for," she said. "That's what they called me at the boarding school Mother and Father sent me to. I was said to be a nimble conversationalist."

"Well I'd say they pegged you about right," said Fargo. "We're due in El Paso tomorrow morning and you still haven't found yourself the fellow you're after. So you're fixing to settle on me."

She leaned forward, reaching across the table to place a hand atop one of his.

"I wouldn't put it that way. I'd have offered you a retainer had I seen you within five minutes of leaving Boston. You have an, oh, I don't know, an aura of rough-hewn ability not often seen in men back East, Mr. Fargo, or in many I've seen out here. You are the man I've been looking for."

That tingling sensation had returned, strange yet pleasant when her palm touched the back of his rough hand there on the table. But it wasn't enough to keep him from thinking clearly.

"Ma'am, you ladies always surprise me, but you're a pip. Our meeting isn't coincidental meeting, is it?"

Her high cheekbones blushed. She indicated a windowed entrance at one end of the dining car behind him. "I'm afraid I did peer in and observe until every other seat was taken except this one." She smiled the merest hint of a smile. "Uh, if you don't mind my saying so, Mr. Fargo, no one seemed desirous of wanting to sit with you."

Fargo glanced about them at the gentrified passengers enjoying their sumptuous repasts and jabbering among themselves while he sat clad in the buckskins of a trailsman, his Colt holstered at his right hip. "Imagine that. Reckon I'm not what these people are looking for."

"Well, I'm not them. You make a strong first impression, Mr. Fargo. My first impression of you is precisely that of the man I have been seeking. And may I add that when it comes to first impressions, mine always prove accurate. Always."

He held up both hands in a friendly, placating manner. "Miss, far be it from me to question anything you say about yourself."

Dinner arrived. The Flyer was noted for its outstanding cuisine, and Fargo's steak was proof enough for him, seasoned and grilled to perfection. There was a natural pause in their conversation as amenities were exchanged over the tastiness of their dinner.

Fargo observed the "lady" attacking her steak as if she hadn't eaten in days, with an intensity of purpose that temporarily precluded conversation. He couldn't help but chuckle again, this time inwardly. He wasn't sure yet if it would be advantageous for him to let Miss Newton of Boston know how much she tickled his fancy. He found her peculiar brand of forthright intelligence and sass extremely appealing, and she was real easy on the eyes. And it counted that it was family business that had brought her to this hostile environment, more than a thousand miles from her home. Fargo had always placed a high value on allegiance to family, which Lara's behavior embodied.

After several minutes of eating, he said between chews, "Tell me about your brother."